That morning in October, Uncle Stoppard shook me awake with one hand and rattled papers under my nose with the other. I was still half asleep. The rustling papers sounded like stiff, leathery bat wings flapping through my bedroom.

I opened a bleary eye. "Bats?" I said.

"Taco," I thought he said.

"I don't want a taco," I mumbled.

"Not taco—*Occo*. Finn, get up."

"It's too early. Too dark out."

"You can sleep on the way to Occo."

I was wide-awake now. "Occo? You mean, as in Africa? What's in Occo?"

"A big, beautiful bird," he said. A grin stretched across Uncle Stoppard's face like a rubber band with teeth. "I've been nominated for the Ruby Raven. The most prestigious, the most exciting, the most coveted award in mysterydom."

"It's big, huh."

"Bigger than the Edgar, the Dagger, the Agatha, the Anthony, the Macavity, and the Shamus all rolled into one. It's worth a million dollars."

Z

THE
R · U · B · Y
RAVEN

A FINNEGAN ZWAKE MYSTERY

MICHAEL DAHL

AN ARCHWAY PAPERBACK
Published by POCKET BOOKS

New York   London   Toronto   Sydney   Singapore

AN ARCHWAY PAPERBACK *Original*

An Archway Paperback published by
POCKET BOOKS, a division of Simon & Schuster Inc.
1230 Avenue of the Americas, New York, NY 10020

ISBN: 0-671-03271-2

First Archway Paperback printing December 1999

10   9   8   7   6   5   4   3   2

AN ARCHWAY PAPERBACK and colophon are
registered trademarks of Simon & Schuster Inc.

Front cover illustration by Lisa Falkenstern

Printed in the U.S.A.

IL 7+

To Kathy Baxter

THE
R • U • B • Y
RaveN

1
The Raven Calls

My family has always had a fondness for dead things.

One of my grandmothers, for instance, was a paleontologist and hunted for fossils. You can see her bones on display in the Smithsonian Museum of Natural History. One of my uncles runs the funeral home in Deadwood, South Dakota. My cousin Andy works the graveyard shift at a Tombstone Pizza factory. Mom's favorite writer is Robert Graves. Dad's favorite band is the Grateful Dead. And because of my family's weird association with dead things, like fossils and tombs and Shakespeare, I ended up in the middle of a raging sandstorm in the middle of the Sahara Desert with Uncle Stoppard, an evil queen, a Russian mummy, a lunatic, and a dead body. I mean, two dead bodies. No, better make that just one body. I'll explain later.

A year ago, last summer, Uncle Stoppard and I discovered our first dead body in the basement. Locked in our storage room. After we helped the police catch the murderer, I thought things were finally going to settle down. But first there was our so-called vacation to Agualar in Central America. Some vacation. Filled with dinosaur hunters, underground caverns, tropical storms and a thousand-year-old knife that could pass through the wall of a tent without making a hole.

We survived the tropical storm, but barely.

At the Mexico City airport, we were greeted by some old friends from the Ackerberg Institute, the same institute that employed my parents as archeologists. The old friends thoughtfully relieved us of an ancient Mayan treasure that we were planning to transport back to the States. Unfortunately, most of our money, or our potential money, was wrapped up in that Mayan treasure. I thought there would be a reward. I was wrong. Our trip to Agualar swallowed up all of our money and most of our summer clothes (which were blown away in the storm). A month after we returned home to Minneapolis, I had to spend the first day of school wearing an old shirt of Uncle Stoppard's, long pants, and stiff black dress shoes we had dug out of the back of the storage locker. But I was glad that school had started. Life was back to normal.

I was wrong. Dead wrong.

Uncle Stoppard woke me up early one morning in October, waving sheets of yellow paper in my face.

"Finn," he said. "Wake up." My full name is Finnegan, but Uncle Stoppard likes nicknames.

To look at us, you'd never guess we were related. Uncle Stoppard is tall and muscular, with wavy red hair, green eyes, and a large nose (he calls it aquiline). I am not tall or muscular. I have light brown hair, pale skin, and freckles, or as Uncle Stoppard puts it, I have a *moccachino* crop, *java* eyes, and a *triple-latte* complexion with *nutmeg sprinkles.* Uncle Stoppard drinks a lot of coffee. He also likes using unusual words.

One thing we share is our glasses. I mean, we both *wear* glasses. And we also share the family fondness for dead things: I like ghost stories and Uncle Stop spends most of his time plotting to kill people. We've been living together about eight years, and I've gotten used to living in his apartment in south Minneapolis. I don't think about my parents as much as I used to. Now I only think about them a couple times a day. They're considered legally dead since they disappeared several years ago while searching for Tquuli the Haunted City hidden somewhere among the frozen volcanoes of Iceland. How do I know my parents are still alive? I just know.

If there's one thing people in my family know, it's when something or someone is dead.

Someday Uncle Stoppard and I are going to fly to Iceland and bring back my parents, but expeditions cost a lot of dead presidents and that's something we don't have. That's what Uncle Stoppard calls money, dead presidents. Because of the faces on dollar bills.

That morning in October, Uncle Stoppard shook me awake with one hand and rattled papers under my nose with the other. I was still half asleep. The rustling papers sounded like stiff, leathery bat wings flapping through my bedroom.

I opened a bleary eye. "Bats?" I said.

"Taco," I thought he said.

"I don't want a taco," I mumbled.

"Not taco—*Occo*. Finn, get up."

"It's too early. Too dark out."

"You can sleep on the way to Occo."

I was wide awake now. "Occo? You mean, as in Africa?" How could we travel across the Atlantic Ocean on the day before a school day?

"I'm surprised you know where it is." Uncle Stoppard sat down on the edge of my bed.

"Occo," I said. "An Arab kingdom on the west coast of Africa sandwiched between the countries of Lesser Occo and Morocco."

"Sandwiched?"

"That's what the geography book says."

"Good memory. Do you know what Occo's nickname is?"

"The Side Door to the Sahara," I said. "And the major export is sand used for baseball diamonds."

"Very impressive, Finn. So why the C in Mr. Hudson's geography test last week?"

I couldn't tell Uncle Stoppard the real reason.

"What's in Occo?" I asked.

"A big, beautiful bird," he said. A grin stretched across Uncle Stoppard's face like a rubber band with teeth. "I've been nominated for the Ruby Raven."

"The Ruby Raven?"

"The most prestigious, the most exciting, the most coveted award in mysterydom."

"It's big, huh?"

"Bigger than the Edgar, the Dagger, the Agatha, the Anthony, the Macavity, and the Shamus all rolled into one."

And those were big awards.

"It's worth a million dollars."

A million? Enough dead presidents to fly us to Iceland and back.

Uncle Stoppard stared at the yellow sheets in his hand. "The letter states that I have to be present to win. So what choice do I have? The ceremony will be held in Occo on the thirteenth. And stop jumping on the bed."

"That's only three days away," I said.

"Less than that," he said. "If you take into account all the time zones and—"

"When do we leave?"

Uncle Stoppard's cucumber-green eyes were staring at something beyond the bedroom wall, thousands of miles away. "The competition is tough," he said. "The authors of the best mysteries from around the world will all be there." He read from the letter. "Lizardo, Neez,

Zamboni—I haven't seen him in a couple of years. Even Ota Sato from Japan."

Uncle Stop writes murder mysteries. That's what I meant about his plotting to kill people. He's published about a dozen books, but his newest, and most famous one, is *Into My Grave*. That's the real controversial one based on William Shakespeare's play *Hamlet*.

Uncle Stop says that *Hamlet* is the greatest play in the English language. It's about this guy named—what else?—Hamlet, who lived four hundred years ago. Hamlet is a prince and his dad is dead. The king's ghost comes back and reveals to Hamlet that he, the king, was murdered. Poisoned by his own brother, Hamlet's uncle, Claude. "Revenge me," says the ghost. "Sure, Dad," says Hamlet. So Prince Hamlet plots to murder his uncle. And to confuse Claude and keep him from suspecting things, Hamlet pretends to be bonkers. You know, crazy.

That's the story Shakespeare tells. Not exactly original.

But Uncle Stoppard had this truly stunning idea to rewrite *Hamlet* as if it were a detective story. And in Uncle Stop's version, Hamlet is the murderer. You see, Hamlets Senior and Junior go for a stroll on the castle roof, get into an argument, and then Hamlet Jr. angrily shoves his dad over the edge. Uncle Stoppard said that since the story takes place in October, the king dies in the fall. Prince Hamlet can't accept his own guilt, so he goes nuts—*really* nuts—and convinces himself that innocent Uncle Claude is the real murderer. So the whole time that Hamlet is plotting to kill his father's killer, he doesn't remember that he himself is the actual killer.

Into My Grave is what people in the mystery biz call a critical success. That means the critics liked it, but not enough normal people bought the book to make Uncle Stoppard rich. Or help him pay his bills. Like cable TV and groceries. The *New York Times* said *Into My Grave* was "Dazzling!" The *Minneapolis Star-Tribune* said "Hypnotic!" The *Des Moines Register* said, "Highly Inventive!" Uncle Stoppard said, "Big deal."

"If the book doesn't sell," he said, "what's the point in writing it? *Into My Grave* isn't for critics, it's for regular people."

He was depressed for weeks. He stopped jogging every morning, stopped working out at the gym, and spent most of his nights planted in front of the TV watching old videos starring dead actors while he and his cop buddy, Jared Lemon-Olsen, scarfed down buckets of Italian ice cream with unpronounceable flavors.

A third-rate actor from England, who claims to be the only living descendant of William Shakespeare, wrote a twenty-page e-mail letter to Uncle Stoppard demanding that he rewrite *Into My Grave*. "Change the story back the way my ancestor wrote it," wrote the Brit. "Hamlet is not a murderer!" (Actually, he is, if you've read the play. There are gobs of dead people lying on the stage in the final scene.) Anyway, the Brit said that Uncle Stoppard had dishonored the most famous name in all of literature. Every week Uncle Stop deletes weird e-mail from the guy.

English teachers, or, I should say, teachers of English, send us hate mail from all over the world. "How dare you revise Shakespeare!" they write (with lots of exclamation points). "He was the greatest playwright who ever lived! Who are you—an American—to change one word? You're not fit to erase Shakespeare's commas!"

How does Uncle Stoppard answer all those exclamation points? "Poetic license," he says. "I'm a writer and Shakespeare's dead." See? That dead stuff again.

Anyway, that Sunday morning in October was the

most excited I had seen Uncle Stoppard in weeks or
months. He handed me one of the yellow sheets to read.
"Notice anything odd, Finn?" he asked.

Stoppard Sterling
Minneapolis, Minnesota U.S.A.

Dear Mr. Sterling:

Congratulations! The Nevermore Society is
pleased to announce that "Into My Grave" has
been selected as a finalist for the 13th Ruby Raven
Award for the World's Best Classic Mystery. The
Award and the Cash Prize of $1 million will be pre-
sented in Occo on October 14. Contestants must
arrive at the Fuz Hôtel Splendide by 12:00 P.M.
(Greenwich Mean Time) on October 13.

YOU MUST BE PRESENT TO WIN.
(Tickets and itinerary are enclosed.)

Sincerely,

Truman Ravenwood
President, Nevermore Society

Nominees:

Bah	Occo	
Kloo	Russia	*Trentsky's Last Case*
Lizardo	Spain	*Footprints on Fiji*
Neez	Egypt	*The Sphinx Bleeds at Dawn*
Sato	Japan	*Deadly Diet*
Sterling	U.S.A.	*Into My Grave*
T.-Squeer	U.K.	*Murder on the Polar Express*
Zamboni	Italy	*Pong Ping of Game Deadly A*

"Well?" he asked.

"Well, Zamboni's title is printed backwards," I said.

"Bah," Uncle Stop said.

"Look, it's backwards."

"No, I mean *Omar* Bah," Uncle Stoppard said. "He's one of the finalists. But he hasn't written anything in years. Look, there's a blank by his name. No title."

I looked again. "Maybe it's a typo," I said. That's a writer's word for mistake.

"Humpffh," snorted Uncle Stop. "He'll probably win."

"Why do you say that?"

"Look where Omar Bah is from. Occo! The award ceremony will probably turn out to be one of those stupid political things. I've heard that Ravenwood character is a little weird, anyway."

"That's not fair," I said. We deserved those million dead presidents. I mean, of course, that Uncle Stoppard deserved them. But we could both use them. To pay rent. Buy groceries. Fly to Iceland. "The prize should go to the best writer," I said. "You!"

Uncle Stoppard snorted again.

I reread the list of nominees. "Oh, there's Mona," I said.

Uncle Stop looked as if he had swallowed a sack of lemons.

"I know," he said. "I was hoping that *she* was a typo. But she'll be there. As usual. Her Royal Highness."

If I didn't do something fast, Uncle Stoppard would start grumbling about Mona Trafalgar-Squeer all the way to Africa.

"Too bad we're not going to Occo," I said, lying back down.

Uncle Stoppard grabbed my covers and hurled them off the bed. "Who says we're not going?"

"Well, since Mona is going to be there, and Mr. Bah is going to win the Ruby Rooster—"

"Ruby Raven."

I knew it had something to do with a bird.

"Into My Grave is a darn good story," Uncle Stoppard said. "I have as much chance of winning that prize as anyone else."

"Exactly," I said.

"Besides, the airplane tickets are free."

I jumped out of bed. "All right, so what do we take to Occo?"

"Your clothes are already packed." He pointed to a green suitcase and travel bag slouching on the floor next to my bed.

"But when—?"

"I packed while you were asleep," Uncle Stoppard said. "And I called a cab. Now, our plane leaves in one hour. Then it's a one-hour flight to Chicago. Ten hours from Chicago to Paris. Overnight in Paris. Leave early the next morning, and five hours later we're in Fuz on the thirteenth."

"Fuzz?"

"The capital of Occo."

"It's pronounced *Fooz,"* I said.

"Which rhymes with *lose,"* he said. "Now, hurry and get dressed, Finn. Our schedule is tight. Especially since we travel through six different time zones. If we miss any of these connections, even one, we won't arrive at the award ceremony on time and I'll blow my chances at getting the Bird."

A small explosion rocked our apartment building. I heard the living room windows shatter as Uncle Stoppard stumbled backwards, tripped over my already-packed suitcase, knocked his head against my closet door, and passed out.

Cold water. That's what the experts say you need for people who pass out.

I jumped over Uncle Stoppard's motionless body, ran into the kitchen and threw open the refrigerator door. No bottled water. Uncle Stoppard must have drunk it all. The only cold liquid was milk. Better than nothing. I rushed back to the bedroom carrying a gallon container, screwed off the pink plastic lid, and dumped the cowjuice on Uncle Stoppard's head.

The experts are right. Uncle Stoppard immediately opened his eyes. He sat up, gasping and sputtering like a landed fish. "What is all this?" he said, wiping at his face.

"Skim," I said.

"What is it doing all over me? Ow!" He grabbed the back of his head.

There was a knock on our back kitchen door. I heard the worried voice of our upstairs neighbor, Joan. "Are you two all right in there?" Joan Bellini was a nurse. She would know what to do. I hopped over Uncle Stoppard a second time and let Joan inside. She was wearing an orange sweatshirt and green sweatpants. Under normal circumstances, Joan was always color coordinated. The explosion must have rattled her, too.

"I'm fine," said Uncle Stoppard as Joan and I helped him to his feet. "And we don't have a lot of time, Finn."

"You have time to sit down here at the table," said Joan. "Drink this glass of water. Is that milk in your hair?"

"Skim," said Uncle Stoppard. His hand shook as he took the glass from Joan.

"What was that noise?" I asked.

"Something blew up," said Joan. "Something outside. Alison went out the front door to find out. I thought I'd check if everyone in the building was okay."

Our back door opened. This time it was our neighbor

from the apartment next door, Pablo de Soto. He was wearing jeans, a white T-shirt, and no shoes.

"Is everyone all right in here?" Pablo asked. "Hey, is that milk?"

Joan's roommate, Alison Brazil, also appeared at the back door. She was breathing hard. "Explosion," she panted. "At the end of the block. A car on fire. Lots of smoke. Broken glass everywhere." She glanced over at Pablo's bare feet. "Watch where you step."

"That's a nasty bump on your head, Mr. Sterling," said Joan.

"Finn," said Uncle Stoppard. "Look out the window and see if our cab is here yet. My luck, it was the cab that exploded."

"That looks like milk in your hair," said Alison.

"Did you say *cab?*" asked Joan.

"Yeah, it's for Africa," I said. I walked down the hall and into the living room. My slippers crunched on broken glass as I stepped over the wooden floor. Books and CDs had been knocked from their shelves. A framed picture of one of Uncle Stoppard's book covers—*Sneezing and Coffin*—had fallen off the dining room wall and lay sideways on the sofa. Cold wind blew through the windows that faced the street, fluttering the curtains. Magazines, scattered on the floor, flipped their pages in the breeze, turned by phantom fingers.

The sidewalks and front yards were thinly covered in white from a snowfall the night before. Down the street, to my right, I saw the car that Alison had described. Thick black clouds and yellow flames billowed up from a blackened metal car frame. Where was the driver? Lots of people were standing around calmly watching the disaster as if it were a made-for-TV movie. One guy was taking pictures with a video camera. Dozens of car alarms had been set off by the blast. They were buzzing and beeping like an army of angry frogs. No sign of a cab. I heard a police siren as I turned from the windows and returned to the kitchen.

Uncle Stoppard was standing next to his chair, looking a little wobbly.

"Mr. Sterling, you're not going anywhere in this condition," Joan said.

"Joan," he said. "What would you do if you had a chance to win a million dollars?"

"A million dollars?" she said.

"A million dollars?" said Pablo.

"A million dollars," said Uncle Stoppard.

The kitchen was silent for three seconds.

"We'll help you pack," said Alison.

"We're already packed," I said.

"Omigosh!" Uncle Stoppard dropped into his chair and slapped himself on the forehead.

"Are you sick?" I asked.

He stared at me. "I packed your stuff, but I forgot to pack mine!"

Uncle Stoppard's bedroom always looks like ground zero after a bomb blast. And not a smart bomb, either. With a little determination, Joan, Alison, Pablo, and I managed to make it look worse. The four of us dug through piles of clothes, yanked shirts out of closets, flung shoes through the air, crammed underwear into suitcases. The whole time Uncle Stoppard, still in his pajama bottoms, still sitting in the kitchen with his head in his hands, kept yelling out orders.

"Not black jeans, they'd be too hot. Find the ecru ones. Ecru. It means beige. Yes, I need at least one flannel shirt, I hear the desert gets cool in the evenings. No, not the red one, the teal one. It's blue-green. Sunglasses! Where are my sunglasses? Finn, can you find my chukka boots? The ones I bought last fall!"

Uncle Stoppard shouldered his way into the room and snatched an old-fashioned tuxedo from his closet. "I only paid twenty bucks for this baby at a garage sale," he said. He rolled the tux into a ball and stuffed it into a carrying bag. Then, while writing a note for our building's caretaker, Ms. Pryce, Uncle Stoppard asked Pablo if he could watch our apartment the rest of the day.

"No problemo," said Pablo.

"And here's the number for Officer Lemon-Olsen. Remember meeting him?" That's Uncle Stoppard's cop buddy, an expert on fingerprints and knives. "If you could call him and tell him about the explosion, he'll probably be able to put some cardboard on our broken windows."

"Don't worry," said Joan. "We'll take care of it. Now, get out of here! You don't want to miss your plane." A few minutes later we carried suitcases, bags, and Uncle Stoppard outside to a waiting yellow cab.

The frosty morning air had grown colder. As I walked around the front of the cab to get in the other side, I saw, striding down the sidewalk to meet us, our landlady, Ms. Pryce. She must have been part of the crowd watching the burning vehicle. Probably roasting marshmallows. "And where are you off to?" she asked.

Uncle Stoppard was silent. He had been avoiding Ms. Pryce for the past two weeks because of our rent problem.

"They're on their way to Africa," said Joan, cheerily.

"Africa?" Ms. Pryce tilted her blue head toward Uncle Stoppard as he crawled into the backseat of the cab. Her head isn't blue, only her hair. Blue like a kindergarten crayon. The rest of her outfit was midnight black, the only color she ever wears. I think Ms. Pryce is one of the undead. You know, a vampire.

She folded her wings, I mean her arms. "I'm always surprised at how some people can take off for vacations anytime they feel like it, but still not pay their rent on time."

Uncle Stoppard had rolled down his window. "This is not a vacation," he explained from the backseat. "Besides, it's paid for."

Ms. Pryce pointed at our apartment. "Well, *that* is not."

"The broken windows aren't our fault," I said.

"I'm talking about the rent," she said.

"Ms. Pryce," said Alison. "This is an emergency."

"Uncle Stoppard," I said. "The plane leaves in half an hour."

Uncle Stoppard leaned forward to the cabdriver. "Quick. The airport."

As the cabdriver backed up his vehicle to avoid the burning car at the other end of the block, Uncle Stop leaned out the window and yelled, "We'll be back in a few days."

Ms. Pryce yelled back. "Don't be surprised if your furniture is in the street."

Uncle Stoppard sighed and sat back on the cushiony seat.

"She can't do that, can she?" I asked. "To our furniture? Because we're a little late with the rent?"

The cabdriver squinted at us in his rearview mirror. "You better be able to pay for this ride," he said. "There are cops at the airport, you know."

Uncle Stoppard dropped a twenty-dollar bill on the front seat. A dead president. The one with the swirly white hair that looks like soft-serve ice cream. "Get us there in fifteen minutes," said Uncle Stop, "and you'll get another one of those."

I leaned back and looked out the window. Above the

houses and leafless trees flying past, I saw a single cold star glittering in the pale purplish sky.

"She can't do that, can she?" I repeated.

Uncle Stoppard snuggled into his seat, tilted his head back and gazed up through the cab's rear window. "Looks like beautiful flying weather," he said.

2
The Queen and the Cobra

We flew to New York, then over the Atlantic (through seven time zones) to Paris. And though Uncle Stoppard had only three days to get to Occo or he'd miss his chance at the bucks and the Bird, he insisted that we stay half a day in the French capital.

"We're going to be late!" I cried.

"Nonsense," said Uncle Stoppard, his aquiline nose buried in some stupid brochure. "We still have until tomorrow morning to arrive in Fuz. It's all in the itinerary. Let's see, I think we'll go to the Picasso exhibit first, and then—"

Uncle Stoppard dragged me through four museums and three art galleries. I saw enough dead stuff to last a lifetime. The next morning we flew to Fuz.

Fuz, the capital of Occo, is where they manufacture lint. They also make funny little slippers with sharp pointy toes. At the Fuz airport gift shop, Uncle Stop hunted for souvenirs and I looked at all the slippers. I was starting to unlace my running shoes so I could try on a pair, when a salesclerk stopped me. Looking embarrassed, he said, "I'm sure they will fit."

"But how—?"

"You can always try them on at home," he said.

"But, I—"

"Please," he said.

What was his problem? Did he think Americans didn't wash their feet?

"How about wearing jelly babies?" said Uncle Stoppard.

"Jelly babies?" I said.

"Djellabahs," he said more distinctly. He held up two long robes with yellow, blue, and orange stripes. They each had a hood and long, floppy sleeves. "They might be handy if we go trekking in the desert."

"We only go trekking *after* the award ceremony," I said.

"Aye aye," he said.

I suggested that Uncle Stoppard also buy a Fuzi pocket dictionary in case we ran into some Occans that, unlike the salesclerk, did not speak English.

"Au contraire," said Uncle Stoppard, patting his jacket pocket. "I still have that French pocket dictionary I picked up in Paris. French is the second language here in Occo. Almost all the Sahara nations speak it."

"Au revoir," Uncle Stoppard said to the clerk.

"Au revoir," the man said with a bow.

We took a taxi—or, as the French call it, a *taxi*—from the airport to the hotel. The city of Fuz looked like a movie set, and each block belonged to a separate movie. Ancient stone buildings with skinny towers and fat golden domes crowded next to gigantic skyscrapers made entirely of windows. Our taxi drove past medieval castles, modern office buildings, smelly gas stations, crumbly stone fortresses, and fancy restaurants where people sat at white metal tables on the sidewalk. The taxi driver braked before a vast building of granite and marble, topped by a brilliant white dome in the shape of an onion. Footmen in long red robes, white gloves, and little red hats helped us out of the taxi, hauled our luggage up the sixteen wide stone steps to the front entrance, led us through the revolving door, and then disappeared.

The lobby of Le Fuz Hôtel Splendide was a mixture of museum and jungle. A sea of shining marble tiles led to the front desk, while thick, green forests of fully grown potted palm trees swayed in the breeze from circular fans high overhead. I could swear I heard monkeys chattering at us from the treetops.

Five desk clerks smiled at us simultaneously. "Ah, Mr. Sterling. There will be a luncheon reception for the mystery writers at noon. And here is your packet." They handed Uncle Stoppard a large, white envelope. "I'm sure you'll want to relax before lunch. We have special rooms for the writers to freshen up in." They handed Uncle Stoppard a key.

The hotel room on the seventeenth floor was bigger than our whole apartment back in Minneapolis. A huge sitting room with chairs, sofas, mirrors, and potted plants led into two enormous bedrooms, each with a gigantic bathroom attached. Everything was pink! Pink carpet, pink wallpaper, pink curtains. A basket of fruit, almost as tall as me, sat in the front entrance. A gold card stuck among the melons and pineapples said "Congratulations!"

"Hey! How did they know you'd pick this room?" I asked.

"I'm sure they didn't," said Uncle Stoppard. "The hotel reserved a block of rooms for all the Ruby Raven nominees. The rooms probably all look alike."

"That's a lot of pink," I said.

Uncle Stoppard was checking through the packet he had been handed at the front desk. "I'm gonna lie down for a sec, Finn. I think the jet lag is catching up to me. Then we need to hurry and get a bite to eat before our first meeting."

"Meeting?"

"In the lobby in less than an hour."

Less than an hour? Then I knew where I was going.

No pink in the bathroom. It was ultramodern, full of steel, glass, and chrome, with mirrors on the wall, ceiling, and inside the shower stall. No matter how new or old-fashioned a bathroom looks, either in Paris, Minnesota, or Occo, there's always one item that always looks the same.

I had been sitting for only a minute when I heard a noise out in the bedroom. A door shutting. Where was Uncle Stoppard going?

"Uncle Stop!"

A bump, followed closely by another bump. Did the fruit basket fall over? I expected to see a pineapple roll into the bathroom.

A thump against the bathroom door. There's a pineapple, all right. I should have locked the door. A black pineapple? A hissing sound filled the bathroom. It was not a fruit, but a long, black, heavy-headed snake that had knocked the door open. The snake gathered itself together, coiling on top of itself. An evil black head rose about a foot off the floor. Tiny black eyes glittered at me. A cobra!

I swallowed hard.

"Uncle Stop!"

The snake hissed angrily, exposing yellow, needle-sharp fangs.

I slowly stood up, pulling my shorts up inch by inch from around my ankles. I was afraid that a sudden move would frighten or anger the cobra. Its shiny black head wavered back and forth. The black eyes never stopped staring at me.

Where was Uncle Stoppard? Had that bump been the sound of his head hitting the floor after the cobra attacked and poisoned him? Where did the snake come from? The fruit basket? Had it been coiled up silently among the bananas and kiwi?

The cobra was on the move. It uncoiled its shiny body and began sliding toward me over the smooth white floor tiles. Should I climb up on the toilet? It wasn't high enough. The cobra's head could rise up at least a foot. The sinks were too far away for me to reach in time.

Behind me stood the chrome-and-glass shower stall. I carefully backed up, never taking my gaze from the dark, slithering creature. I calmly lifted my right foot over the porcelain border and into the shower. Then the left foot. The cobra kept sliding closer. A red tongue darted out of its mouth like a tiny electric wire.

Bang! I slid the glass door shut. The cobra rushed toward me and then reared itself up, inches from the glass. It hissed at me. I quickly glanced around the shower stall. The doors were too high for the cobra to climb over.

"Uncle Stoppard!" I yelled again. Was he lying dead on the pink bedspread in the other room? Why else didn't he answer me?

At least I was safe inside the stall. The cobra kept staring at me through the glass door. How had it gotten in here?

A bell tinkled somewhere in the other room. Or was that how an Occan telephone sounded? It might have been the elevator out in the hallway. Another tinkle. A bell, like a small dinner bell, was ringing somewhere in one of our bedrooms.

The cobra lowered its head to the floor and slithered toward the bathroom door. Had it heard the bell, too? I thought all snakes were deaf. The black tail of the cobra slid out of sight, behind the corner of the door.

I didn't move a finger. Someone was in the other

room. So was the cobra. The deadly creature might rush back as soon as I opened the shower door.

How long should I wait? Poison could be seeping through Uncle Stoppard's veins. He might need medical attention. There must be a doctor in the hotel. If I waited too long, Uncle Stoppard could die.

"Uncle Stop!"

"Yes, Finnegan?"

Uncle Stoppard was standing in the doorway.

"The cobra!"

"Cobra?"

I stepped out of the shower stall and rushed to the doorway. "There's a cobra out in the bedroom."

Uncle Stop's gaze traveled slowly around the room. "Uh, no, Finn, there isn't. Are you sure you shouldn't lie down for a bit? I think you've got jet lag, too."

"But I saw it. Hey, where did you go?"

"I was only gone for a minute, Finn. I was looking for ice."

"The fruit basket. Did it fall over?"

I peered into the pink bedroom from the safety of the bathroom. No fallen pineapples, no strange bell, no cobra.

"Fruit basket?" said Uncle Stoppard. "Cobra?"

"It was a black cobra, Uncle Stop. Long and black and—"

"And I only had a shriveled apple and a hard bagel on the plane for breakfast," he said. "Let's go look for a place to eat."

The cool, air-conditioned elevator woke me up as we descended to the main lobby. Maybe I had been dreaming. But I'd never dreamed in a sitting position before.

We wandered the jungle-lobby, searching for signs of a coffee shop or restaurant. From behind one of the potted palms stepped a young man in a canary yellow suit.

He looked like a model from one of Uncle Stoppard's *GQ* magazines. He had warm brown eyes behind yellow-framed glasses, a warm smile, and a mocha complexion. With his hat and suit and fancy two-toned shoes, he reminded me of a detective from an old-time movie.

"Stoppard Sterling?" asked the man, taking off his yellow hat. His black hair was plastered flat against his skull, parted in the middle and gleaming like ink.

"That's right," said Uncle Stoppard.

"Here for the award ceremony?"

"Right again," said Uncle Stop.

"Are you not afraid of another attack?" said the man.

"Attack?" I said.

"What are you talking about?" asked Uncle Stoppard.

The guy handed my uncle a folded-up newspaper. Uncle Stoppard took one look at the front page, dropped his jaw, and then handed it to me. The newspaper, not his jaw.

I couldn't believe my eyes. There was a photo of me and Uncle Stop boarding our plane back in Minneapolis. The headline ran, "Famous Author Flees Mysterious Bomber." Below the picture was printed, "Author Stoppard Sterling and an unidentified boy."

"There must be some mistake," Uncle Stoppard said.

"There's a mistake all right," I said. "I didn't get my name in the paper." I was a UFO. An unidentified fleeing object.

"I don't know anything about this," Uncle Stoppard said.

"You don't?" said the man. "Let me introduce myself. I am Abou ben Wittgenstein. I'm a reporter."

Abou (it rhymes with *kazoo*) explained that Uncle Stoppard (and the unidentified boy) were making the international news. There had been an attack on Uncle Stoppard's life. Someone had sent him a time bomb through the mail. Luckily, it exploded in the delivery car before it reached his house. I mean, our house. I mean, unluckily.

"Who sent it?" Uncle Stoppard asked.

"No one knows," Abou said.

"Probably some crank," Uncle Stoppard said.

"We saw the explosion," I said. "Was the mailman hurt?"

"Mail *carrier,*" Uncle Stoppard said to me.

Abou shook his head. "No, she wasn't. According to the paper, she was standing on someone else's front steps when the car blew up."

"If everything blew up," said Uncle Stoppard, "why do people think the bomb was intended for me?"

"Well, according to the news service, there was a small scrap of an address left on the package," said Abou, "with your initials: S.S."

"That could be anyone," said Uncle Stoppard.

"And you are the only celebrity that lives in that neighborhood," added Abou.

"Was it dynamite?" I asked.

"Um, fertilizer," Abou said. Like those terrorist bombs I had seen on TV. Fertilizer bombs were cheap and easy to make. It must have been a big package.

"Why," Uncle Stop asked, "would anyone want to kill me?"

"Perhaps it's an English teacher who didn't like *Into My Grave.*" Abou smiled.

"Like the dart," I said.

"Oh, Finn—"

"What dart?" Abou asked.

Uncle Stoppard looked embarrassed. "It's nothing. Some idiot sent me a dart through the mail."

"A poison dart," I added.

"I never heard about that," Abou said.

"We never reported it to the police," Uncle Stoppard said. "I figured it was some nutcase who didn't like the book. Or some weirdo with too much time on his hands."

"It came in a package that was all wrapped up like a birthday present," I said. "And when Uncle Stoppard opened the lid, the dart went *sproiiiing* and stuck to the ceiling."

"*Sproiiiing?*" Abou said.

"I was fortunate enough to be out of the line of fire," Uncle Stoppard said.

"He tripped," I said.

"Why did you think it was poisoned?" Abou said.

"It *was* poisoned," I said.

"We noticed a strange-looking stain on the steel tip of the dart," said Uncle Stoppard, "So I sent it to the University of Minnesota to be analyzed. It was a lethal dose of nicotine."

"Nicotine? As in cigarettes?"

"There was a famous murder case in Durham, England, last year," Uncle Stoppard said. "A woman used ordinary cigars to make a poison that she slipped into her husband's tea. He died almost instantly."

Abou looked alarmed. "Gosh, and you did not report this to the police?"

"Uncle Stoppard forgot," I said.

"Poison and bombs!" Abou whistled. "Sounds like one of your stories, Mr. Sterling. I've read them all, you know, and—"

I nudged Uncle Stoppard with my elbow. "Ow! Uh, actually we're sort of in a hungry. I mean, in a hurry, Mr. Wittgenstein."

"Call me Abou. And I'm sorry, Mr. Sterling. I did not

mean to bother you. But, well, you see, *Peephole* wants me to do a cover story on you. Photos. Excerpts from your book. That's why I'm here. It would be great publicity."

"*Peephole* magazine!" said Uncle Stoppard.

"Where's your camera?" I asked.

"Mr. Wittgenstone!"

A woman came rushing toward us. Her shiny high heels chattered over the marble floor of the lobby like hailstones.

Uncle Stoppard groaned.

The woman had dark brown hair, almost black, that sloped around her head like a football helmet. How did she get her hair that stiff? Her blue skirt and blue blazer were so bright they hurt my eyes. She didn't wear any jewelry, but a single white rose (a real one!) was pinned to her lapel, matching her icy white blouse and white shoes. From her mouth hung a dainty black cigarette with a golden tip that sent purple puffs of smoke up toward the ceiling fans.

I recognized her from her book jacket photos. It was the Queen herself.

Mona Trafalgar-Squeer is probably the most stunning mystery writer in the world. After Uncle Stoppard, of course. Critics call her the Queen of Crime, the Princess of Puzzles, the Baroness of Bafflement. Her detective hero is the super intelligent Revelation-of-St.-John Bugloop, the half-French, half-Pygmy ex-priest with a trained meerkat for an assistant. He got his weird first name from the missionary nuns who taught him to read and write French. Bugloop's arch nemesis is the one-eyed, seven-foot-tall Duchess of DeMonica, who circles the globe searching for a gem the exact color of her good eye. Mona's plots are amazing. You can never solve her puzzles until you read the last page. Sometimes, not until you read the last word! Mona is a British citizen, but she lives half the year in Minneapolis, where she tools around on a silver Kawasaki, or spends months locked in her apartment overlooking the Mississippi River. Although they both write mysteries and live in the same city, for some unknown reason she and Uncle Stoppard do not get along.

"Queen of Crime?" Uncle Stoppard once said. "Ha! It's a crime her books sell."

While flying from Paris to Fuz, Uncle Stoppard had noticed one of the other plane passengers reading a Trafalgar-Squeer paperback. That pushed him into one of his anti-Mona rants. "She never gives her readers enough clues. Who, for instance, would know that the Malaysian blue tree frog becomes poisonous one month out of the year? One month!" (That's how Mona kills off her victims in *See How They Croak*.) "If she had called it a Malaysian blue tree frog her readers might have looked it up in the encyclopedia. But no—she had to call it by its Malaysian name: *rata guri nuu*. That's not playing fair."

"But Revelation Bugloop mentioned a Malaysian frogologist in chapter ten when he—"

"Impossible clues!" Uncle Stoppard had said.

"People like to be tricked," I pointed out. My favorite book of Mona's is called *Death Ties the Knot*, where the Duchess of DeMonica sews a live boa constrictor into a scarf and then gives the scarf to her victims as a gift. That's the reason I got the C in Mr. Hudson's class. The night before our final test I stayed up until two o'clock in the morning with Mona's book instead of with my geography notes. I had to find out how Revelation Bugloop would unravel the evil duchess's knot. So, technically, the C in Geography is Mona's fault.

The Queen of Crime reached out and shook Abou's hand.

"Mr. Wittgenstone," she said, "I'm so glad you're not late for our interview. I did overhear you say that you're from *Peephole* magazine, didn't I?"

This was the first time I'd ever seen a real, live author up close. Except for Uncle Stoppard, of course. The creator of Revelation-of-St.-John Bugloop, the world's greatest detective, stood puffing on a cigarette a mere three feet away from me. And a wrinkled paperback copy of her boa constrictor book (I had reread it on the plane while Uncle Stoppard snoozed) was squeezed into my backpack, waiting for her autograph. How could I get her signature without hurting Uncle Stoppard's feelings?

"Miss Trafalgar-Squeer," Abou said, nervously replacing and tipping his yellow hat to her. "I was about to call you. I was talking with— This is Mr. Stoppard, uh, Mr. Sterling. Have you two met? Of course you have, being the two front-runners for the Ruby Raven."

Mona glanced quickly at Uncle Stoppard and took a purple puff of her cigarette. I wondered if anyone had told Mona about the Durham Nicotine Murder Case.

"Front-runner?" she said. "Stoppard is considered a front-runner? Using a four-hundred-year-old story that was written by someone else?"

"Good question, Mr. Sterling," Abou said. "What gave you the inspiration to steal, er, borrow the plot from *Hamlet?*"

"I was attacked by a pack of great Danes," said Uncle Stoppard.

"What?" said Abou.

"Uncle Stoppard and I were in the library," I said. "And I accidentally dropped a gigantic book on his foot."

"An old volume of Danish history," Uncle Stoppard

said, "which included the story of the historical Prince Hamlet. The same story that originally inspired Shakespeare."

"You need to be more careful about dropping things, kid," said Mona, looking down at me. "Next time, aim."

"What gave you the idea to make Hamlet's girlfriend the detective?" Abou asked.

Uncle Stoppard looked pleased. "Well—"

"That was your biggest mistake," Mona said. "Anyone who's ever read *Hamlet,* or seen it performed onstage, or watched the movie versions, knows that Ophelia drowns."

"Ah, but in Shakespeare's original written version, the audience only *hears* about Ophelia drowning," Uncle Stoppard said. "They never actually see it happen onstage."

"There was a witness," Mona said, "Queen Gertrude sees her die in the fourth act, remember?"

"When I read *Hamlet,*" Uncle Stoppard said, ignoring Mona and turning to Abou, "I asked myself, What if Queen Gertrude had been tricked? What if Ophelia had only pretended to die? Then I asked myself, What if Ophelia had faked her death?"

"That's the most ridiculous part of your whole plot," Mona jumped in again. "You drag Ophelia back into the story disguised"—puff—"as someone named Osric. Osric?" She laughed and clicked her bloodred fingernails. "Stoppard, haven't you heard? No one uses that old trick any more. Disguises and fake identities went out fifty years ago with Agatha Christie."

I liked Agatha Christie.

"Did they?" Uncle Stop said. "Then I assume you haven't read *Vane Pursuit* by Charlotte MacLeod? Or *Naked Once More* by Peters? Or *The Christie Caper* by Hart? Or *Zombies of the Gene Pool?*"

"Excuse me, Miss Squeer," I said.

"That's Trafalgar-Squeer, kid."

"Have you ever met a real live Pygmy?" I asked.

"You mean like Bugloop?" Mona sucked on her cigarette. "My books are based on imagination and thoroughly documented research. I don't confuse my readers with facts."

"I'll say," Uncle Stop said. *"Rata guri nuu?"*

Mona smiled at him. "You're just sore you didn't think of it first." Then she turned to Abou and said, "Mr. Wittgenstone, let's go somewhere quieter for my interview."

"He's here to interview Uncle Stoppard," I said.

"What?" said Mona.

Abou was sweating. "Well, uh, with the bomb attack on Mr. Sterling's life—"

"Bomb attack?" Mona asked. "What on earth are you talking about?"

I handed her the newspaper.

"It seems, Mona," said Uncle Stoppard, "that someone sent me an exploding package through the mail. That wasn't your idea, was it?"

"I wish it were," she said. "But whoever sent it"—puff—"obviously has taste."

"Agatha Christie, William Shakespeare, and Stoppard Sterling," Abou said. "Three dead authors . . . er, almost dead authors."

"This is all thrilling, I'm sure," Mona said, throwing the newspaper back at Uncle Stop, "but about that interview—"

"Oh, you'll still be in our next issue," Abou said.

"You bet I will," she said.

"We have a section on the back page called *Tantalizing Tidbits* and—"

The color of Mona's face started to match her suit.

"Tidbit!" Purplish smoke shot from her mouth like dragon fire. I was expecting the rose pinned to her blazer to burst into flame. "Tidbit? Listen, Mr. Boo-boo Wittgenface, I am not a tidbit! I am the Queem of Crine. I mean the Creen of Quime. I mean the Queen of Crime."

"Now, now, Mona," said Uncle Stoppard. "Isn't one title enough?"

Mona sputtered at Abou. "Your interview with this, this—" she jabbed her cigarette toward Uncle Stoppard "—this third-rate hack will be the last one you ever write for that noserag of a magazine. I'm going to phone your editor. Your *former* editor—"

The Queem of Crine froze in mid-sentence. A loud-speaker had blared to life from somewhere behind the gigantic potted palms.

"Will the writers for the Ruby Raven award ceremony please come to the front desk? There has been a change in the schedule of events."

Mona turned and marched rapidly across the marble sea. Listening to her clattering heels, I realized I was glad that I hadn't gotten a chance to ask for an autograph.

3
Crackpot

At the front desk, the five clerks directed us to a dim, shadowy clearing within the forest of giant palms. Several distinguished-looking figures had gathered around a strange-looking little man. Among the hubbub of male and female voices confronting the little man, his high, nasal voice pierced the air like the crackle of static electricity. "All shall be explained as soon as I have everyone's undivided attention, thank you," he said. His bright gray eyes, staring out from beneath shaggy blond eyebrows, darted back and forth in his head like a marionette's eyes, back and forth, back and forth, silencing everyone with his spooky, serious gaze. He dressed like a marionette, too, or I mean, like a ventriloquist's dummy, in a pale blue suit. His red polka-dot bow tie did not move as he swiveled his head around, observing the faces in his small audience.

"Please answer as I call your name," said the marionette.

"Who's that?" I whispered to Uncle Stoppard.

The marionette's gray eyes bulged at me. "Did I call your name, young man?"

I was so startled that I couldn't speak. I shook my head.

"Omar Bah?" called the little man, reading from a clipboard.

"Oui!" Omar Bah had a thick, black beard that flowed down over a broad chest. He was only as tall as Uncle Stoppard, but his beard made him look somehow bigger, more impressive. A magnificent robe of emerald silk partially covered his creamy vanilla suit, and a tiny green fooz perched on his head. A fooz, the national hat of Occo, looks like a small, upturned ice-cream bucket. Omar Bah's black eyes gleamed behind tiny gold-rimmed glasses. At first I thought a bat had landed on his face. Then I realized it was his mustache. What a wingspan! The bristles were black and shiny as shoe polish. The points were daggers. It wasn't a mustache, it was a deadly weapon. I remembered what Uncle Stoppard had said back in our apartment in Minneapolis, staring at the telegram that listed the nominees for the Ruby Raven. Why didn't a book title appear after Bah's name? Was it a typo, or something more?

"Nada Kloo?" called the marionette.

People swung around, looking over their shoulders. No answer.

"Babette Lizardo?"

"Si!" A cheerful, plump woman sitting on a plump, comfy-looking sofa raised her hand. Masses of reddish gold curls were tucked under her big, floppy straw hat. So this was Babette Lizardo. I knew that Uncle Stoppard read her books back home. She lived in Barcelona, on the coast of Spain, and was once dubbed the Queen of Crime. Before Mona came along, that is. Now, Babette is known as the *Spanish* Queen of Crime. Babette's spooky mysteries each take place in a different, exotic location. One of her books, *Bloodstains in Belize,* was made into a miniseries on American TV last year, starring that new Mexican rock star. Her books have plenty of suspense and adventure, but they don't have much blood in them. Babette's glowing pink ears and

wrists and neck were covered by gobs of gold jewelry, which tinkled whenever she shifted her weight. Her necklaces were made of tiny gold question marks.

After her name was called, Babette turned to Uncle Stoppard and winked at him.

"Nabi Neez?" the little man read off his clipboard.

"Upstairs in his room, I believe," said Babette.

The little man was not pleased. He wrote something next to Nabi Neez's name. "Ota Sato?" he called.

A slender, bespectacled Asian man in a brownish suit bowed.

"That's Ota Sato?" I whispered to Uncle Stoppard. "I thought you said he was a sumo wrestler." This time I made sure the little man in the bow tie couldn't hear me. But Abou heard me.

"Sato is an ex-sumo," Abou whispered back. "See the white belt he wears?"

"How could you miss it?"

"He always wears white belts, to remind him—and everybody else—of his former sumo white belt, worn only by grand champions."

"He was a grand champion?"

"Japanese sports fans love him! He's also famous for his diet books and exercise videos."

Sumo wrestlers were mountains of muscle and flesh. Sato must have lost more than 250 pounds since his wrestling days. I'll bet people paid a fat sum to learn his diet secrets.

"It is rather remarkable that he was nominated for the Ruby Raven," Abou added. "This is his first mystery."

"What? Oh, yes. I'm here," said Uncle Stoppard. Uncle Stop had been half listening to me and Abou whispering behind his back when the bow-tied marionette called out his name.

Babette Lizardo snorted when Mona's name was called. Then the little man reached the last name on his clipboard. "Brentano Zamboni?"

"He's not here, either," said Babette. "He went sightseeing."

The marionette eyes darted back and forth again. He set his clipboard on a low glass table, then straightened his tie. "I am Mr. Hyde," he said. "Personal assistant to Truman Ravenwood. There has been a change in plans. The award ceremony that was to take place here at the hotel this evening has been moved. Due to some bombings in the city—"

"Bombings?" said Babette.

"Anti-Japanese terrorists," said Mr. Hyde.

Were the people of Occo protesting the nomination of Ota Sato for the Ruby Raven award?

"For safety reasons," continued Mr. Hyde, "Mr. Ravenwood has decided to move the ceremony to his own residence in Aznac. It's several hours east of here, in the Sahara. Transportation will be provided by Mr. Ravenwood, of course. Please be back here in the lobby in two hours, ready to—"

A loud crack split the air. A bomb? I looked up toward the high glass ceiling and saw palm leaves swaying in the breeze created by the electric fans. One tree was swaying a little too wide.

"Look out!" yelled Mona.

With a great whooshing sound, one of the potted palms crashed to the marble floor. The heavy trunk smashed onto the glass table and the sofa, sending dust, glass, and splinters of wood flying through the air. A few loosened coconuts rolled across the floor.

Terrorists?

"Babette!" screamed Mona. "Where's Babette?"

A plump arm covered in gold bangles and rings fluttered out from under one of the wide palm leaves. "Assistance, please!" came a weak voice.

Ota Sato and Omar Bah helped Babette to her feet. Luckily, she hadn't been crushed by the heavy tree. When she spied the falling trunk, the Spanish Queen of Crime had vaulted behind the sofa like an Olympic diver. I'm glad Mona had screamed. The palm that fell had been standing directly behind Abou. Without Mona's alarm, we wouldn't have seen the tree toppling until it was too late.

Where was Abou?

"This is intolerable!" Mr. Hyde had gotten to his feet, his bow tie looped over one ear, and was brushing dust off his pale blue suit.

The desk clerks and several security guards in long red robes, that barely hid the guns and billy clubs swinging from their belts, rushed over to help. A crowd of hotel guests also swarmed around us, oohing and aahing. I was reminded of our neighbors back in Minneapolis watching the burning remains of the exploded mail car.

"A terrible accident," the desk clerks were saying. "Terrible. No one is hurt? Wonderful. Praise be to Allah, you are safe. Wonderful. This is terrible, simply terrible."

Two guards were examining the large ceramic pot that the palm had been standing in only minutes before. A wide crack had split the pot, spilling dirt and roots onto the marble tiled floor and loosening the giant tree. Abou was speaking with the guards.

"Odd," said Uncle Stoppard.

"That the tree fell?" I said.

"That it fell in our direction," he said.

"The pot simply broke apart," said Abou, joining us among the wreckage. "Probably a flaw in the design. The guards told me the trees were delivered last week."

"Last week?" said Uncle Stoppard.

"This is a brand-new hotel, you know."

"But it looks ancient," I said.

"It was designed to look that way," said Abou. "This is one of our newest buildings, built by Japanese wealth. Each month brings a new wave of Japanese businessmen. Many Occans are growing tired or angry with the many skyscrapers going up each week, destroying the beauty of their, um, *our* ancient city. The owners of Hôtel Splendide thought it best if their building blended in with the old Fuzi traditions."

How did Abou know so much? And then, almost as if he could read my mind, Abou added with a smile, "I'm a reporter, remember?"

Weird, that the ceramic pot would choose that exact moment to break apart, when the mystery writers were gathered nearby. And weird that the palm tree would fall, as Uncle Stoppard said, in our direction.

"Abou," said Uncle Stoppard. "What did Hyde mean about the anti-Japanese terrorists?"

By this time, the mystery writers had calmed down and gone their separate ways. The crowd was beginning to break up. Mr. Hyde was ranting at the desk clerks, while the three of us had moved away from the horizontal tree and were sitting on some purple velvet chairs near the front entrance. I kept an eye on our luggage, which still sat by the front desk.

"There have been reports of a bombing downtown, at one of the newer skyscrapers," said Abou. "I heard it on the radio as I drove over here. As I say, some Occans dislike foreigners coming to our country, bringing new ways, changing things. Even if the foreigners bring money."

How did Ota Sato, ex-sumo wrestler turned mystery writer, feel about staying in a country where he was so intensely disliked? On the other hand, he could walk anywhere in Fuz and see beautiful buildings created by his countrymen. Did he have relatives or friends living here?

"Are you still hungry?" Abou asked.

"Starving," Uncle Stoppard said.

"Me, too," I said.

Abou led us outside the hotel and into the brilliant Occo morning. Paris had been cold and rainy like Minneapolis, but Fuz was hot. The air burned like heat off a stove. Buildings and palm trees only a block away wiggled and quivered in the heat. How could we walk anywhere in this boiling city? The soles of my running shoes would melt and stick to the sidewalk.

At the bottom of the hotel's front steps, Abou waved toward a car.

"Cool!" said Uncle Stoppard. "A Ferlinghetti-Ginzberg!"

The sleek convertible sports car was the same canary yellow as Abou's suit and hat.

"It's one of three in the entire world," Abou said proudly. "Care for a spin, Mr. Sterling?"

"We need to be back here by one o'clock," I said.

"That's more than two hours," Abou said. "Besides, you need to eat."

There must not be a speed limit in Fuz, considering the way Abou burned rubber. I held on to my glasses with both hands to keep them from blowing off my face. How did Abou's hat stay on his head?

Abou ben Wittgenstein, 50 percent Occan and 50 percent German, was a 200 percent mystery fan. Uncle Stoppard, he told us, was his favorite writer. He had read all of Uncle Stop's books and hoped to become a mystery author himself some day. Abou was in his second year of college (studying Shakespeare in Oxford,

England), but was taking a break from school to visit his mom's relatives in Fuz and to write for the Occan branch of *Peephole* magazine, where his dad got him a job. Abou's father, the famous Max Wittgenstein, owned several newspapers back in London, and he wanted his son to get some practical experience in the business. Yesterday, Abou was at the Fuz airport, interviewing people about the anti-Japanese bombings, when he noticed Mona Trafalgar-Squeer and her notorious purple cigarette smoke. Minutes later, he recognized a second famous mystery writer, the Egyptian Nabi Neez. Abou smelled a story. He called his editor at *Peephole,* and the editor, knowing that the mysterious Truman Raven-wood had recently moved to Aznac, guessed that people were arriving for the Ruby Raven awards. No newspapers or television networks are contacted by the Nevermore Society until *after* the award ceremony, so Abou was excited about getting the story first, or, as he called it, "copping a scoop."

Abou snooped around all the hotels and restaurants in Fuz, keeping his eyes peeled for his favorite writer. That's how he ran into us. I think Uncle Stoppard liked the flattery. He rarely talks face to face with his fans. Except me, of course. And I'm his biggest fan.

"Here's Mom's place," Abou said. I had expected a house, but instead, Abou had driven up to a red-and-orange fast-food joint with a gold neon minaret blinking over the parking lot. "We'll do drive-through," he said.

Abou's mother, Lallah Oolah, an Arabic princess, is the founder of the world's first Arabic fast-food restaurant (it's called Burger Sheik—"Home of the World Famous Ali Baba Burger on the Open Sesame-Seed Bun"). We ordered burgers, French Foreign Legion fries, and three shakes: chocolate, coffee, and banana-red pepper. After sitting in Abou's convertible, waiting in line for our orders, with the blazing Occan sun turning the top of my head into a baked potato, the chocolate shake was the best I'd ever tasted.

Uncle Stoppard munched thoughtfully. "I thought Muslims didn't eat beef."

"Actually they don't eat pork," Abou said. "But these burgers are made from soybeans and tofu."

After leaving the Burger Sheik parking lot we drove onto a crowded street that followed an endless brick wall. Camels, taxicabs, sweaty tourists with cameras slung around their necks, and Occan women in hooded black robes slowly strolled alongside our car. I felt as if we were part of a slow-motion parade. Abou pointed to the top of the wall. "The governors of ancient Fuz used to stick the heads of executed criminals up there on wooden posts."

"Charming," said Uncle Stoppard.

I squinted up at the red bricks and the bright blue sky. "I don't see any heads."

"That was hundreds of years ago, Finn."

"Too bad. I've always wanted to see a real live skull," I said, slurping my malt.

"Like poor Yorick, huh?" Abou said.

"Yorick?"

"The fellow whose skull Prince Hamlet finds in the royal cemetery. 'Alas, poor Yorick. I knew him, Horatio: a fellow of infinite jest.' "

"Act Five, Scene One," Uncle Stoppard said.

"Chapter seventeen of *Into My Grave*," Abou said. "Could I steal one of your fries?"

"Remember, we need to get back by one o'clock," I said.

"Hey! I thought of another place. Hold on to this." Abou handed his yellow hat to Uncle Stoppard and gripped the steering wheel tighter. The Ferlinghetti-

Ginzberg made an abrupt right turn, passed through a small archway in the wall, cruised onto a larger, less-crowded street, then shot forward like a bullet.

Here's a creepy thought. Not about skulls or chopped-off heads, but about Abou. What did Uncle Stoppard and I know about him? I mean, what if Abou was the guy who mailed the bomb to our house back in Minneapolis and then followed us here? What if he was pretending to be a big fan of Uncle Stoppard? Pretending be a magazine reporter? I still hadn't seen his camera, or any official identification.

I glanced at the back of Abou's head. He winked at me in the rearview mirror. He looked like a movie star, with his model's smile and his yellow suit and his cool car, not like a mad bomber. Why was I thinking this? I suddenly felt tired and laid my head back on the soft orange leather seat. My body hadn't adjusted to all the time zones yet. It still thought it was 4:30 A.M. back in Minneapolis. Besides, if Abou was the bomber, he could have handed us a time bomb in a fruit basket back in the hotel lobby, said "Love your books!" and then scurried away with his fingers plugged in his ears. The explosion would have been blamed on the anti-Japanese terrorist guys. Mad bombers don't treat you to breakfast and then show you the town.

Unless he had changed his strategy. Maybe he was going to drive us to a lonely, deserted spot where nobody would find our bodies. Maybe our heads would end up stuck on wooden posts like grisly popcorn balls.

The highway—or, as the French call it, *le highway* (not really)—swung around to the north toward some rocky foothills. As we raced farther and farther from downtown Fuz, blue mountains rose up on our right. Beyond them, I knew, lay the Sahara Desert and Aznac and Truman Ravenwood. Abou was steering toward what looked like a gigantic castle perched on the side of a hill. As we drove closer, the "castle" turned out to be hundreds and hundreds of separate stone buildings built on top of each other.

"The Mallomar Tombs," Abou announced.

Not only were the tombs old (Abou said they were built before Columbus was a baby), but they were huge. I mean, *huge*. You'd think they contained dead elephants instead of dead Mallomars. The Mallomars were a royal family that ruled Occo, Lesser Occo, and Morocco in the thirteenth century. Busy folks. Most of them were two or three stories tall. The tombs, I mean, not the Mallomars. And there were lots of them, too—too many to count—scattered all over the rocky hills. They were built out of bricks and thousand-year-old bathroom tiles of pink, orange, gold, and blue. The tombs were built so closely together that they seemed to be holding each other up by the shoulders.

Uncle Stop called them "department buildings for the departed." Abou laughed. I shivered. The Occan sun was bright, but there were deep, dark shadows in the cracks and narrow alleys that ran between the tombs.

This was the perfect place to tell ghost stories—or murder someone.

4
Pushing the Pillar

Since the ancient Mallomars had built their tombs on the high hills north of Fuz, we had a great view of the city, spread out like a colorful, lumpy carpet to our south. "This way you can say that you've seen everything," Abou said.

The Ferlinghetti-Ginzberg parked next to a small tour van. Abou was about to take his hat back when he noticed Uncle Stoppard admiring it. "Try it on, Mr. Sterling. Ah, yes, yellow is definitely your color." I thought the color made Uncle Stoppard look like he had indigestion, but that could have been due to Abou's driving.

The *Peephole* reporter spread his arms dramatically. "Here is where many sultans and sultans' wives began their pilgrimage to the Farthest Mosque."

"Is that in Moscow?" I asked.

Abou gazed up at the bright sky. "No, it is a bit farther."

Gravel crunched beneath our feet in the parking lot. We could see, about a hundred yards away, people walking among the tombs. They looked like tiny dolls next to the huge stone structures. Uncle Stoppard waved to one of the dolls, but it disappeared into a crack between the buildings.

"I could have sworn that was Brent Zamboni," he said.

Abou squinted at the distant crack. "The same Zamboni who wrote *The Maltese Microchip?*"

"Stoppard, darling!" It was Babette Lizardo. She threw two plump arms around Uncle Stoppard's neck and kissed him on both cheeks. "Wasn't it awful? I could have been flattened like a tortilla!"

"You moved pretty fast back there, Miss Lizardo," I said.

Babette laughed brightly, her earrings tinkling. "Not as fast as Mr. Hyde."

"Excuse me, Babette," said Uncle Stoppard. "But how did you get here?"

"The hotel organized a mini-excursion for those interested. Ota Sato is here, too. I think this is where Mr. Zamboni planned to do some sightseeing, as well. And who is this charming creature?" Babette bent down to look at me. "Your son?"

"Oh, no," Uncle Stoppard said. "This is my nephew Finn. Finnegan Zwake."

"Zwake?" Babette put a finger to her lips. "I remember reading about some explorers by that name. They disappeared a few years back."

"Those were—I mean, *are*—my parents," I said.

"Extraordinary," Babette said. "Leonardo and Anna Zwake. Marvelous people. Beautiful mother. Photographed nicely, I remember. Didn't they discover a new Sphinx in Egypt?"

"It may have been new to them, but it was not new to *us.*"

This was said by a tall, skinny man who stood a few feet from Babette. His voice was stern, but the spark in his eyes made me think he might start laughing at any moment. He had honey-colored skin, wore a red-and-gold striped djellabah, a matching hat, and a pair of new blue tennis shoes. His shoes reminded me of Uncle

Stoppard's book *Cold Feet,* where the killer always leaves a pair of blue shoes next to the dead bodies of his victims.

"Forgive my lack of manners," Babette said. "Stoppard Sterling, Finnegan Zwake, this is Nabi Neez of Egypt."

Uncle Stoppard grabbed the man's hand and shook it warmly. "Mr. Neez, I've read your Scientific Detective series, and I think it's terrific."

Nabi Neez bowed. "I did not think I was read outside the Islamic world."

"Not read widely enough, that's true," Uncle Stoppard said. "But Brentano Zamboni—"

"The Italian writer?"

"Yes. He's a friend of mine, an e-mail friend. He sends me translations of all sorts of books and magazines over the Internet that I normally can't find in the States."

"Here is my latest," said Nabi. He produced a thick paperback from beneath his voluminous djellabah and handed it to Uncle Stoppard. Then he pulled out another copy for Abou and another one for me. *The Case of the Cairo Gyro.*

While Nabi Neez was autographing our books, I mean, his books, Babette herded the five of us toward the entrance to the Mallomar cemetery. We stopped beneath an immense stone archway. It looked like the Arc de Triomphe that Uncle Stoppard and I had seen in Paris yesterday.

"How high is this?" I asked. *This, this, this.* My words echoed off the high ceiling.

"Five stories," Abou said. "The colored tiles up there on the ceiling are arranged to look like constellations in the Occan sky."

A dark smudge covered one corner of the ceiling. "Is that supposed to be a black hole?" I asked.

"Those are bats," Abou said.

"Bats?" yelped Uncle Stoppard.

"Pyramid bats we call them back home," Nabi said. "Or *Rhinopomidae rhinopoma*, to put it more precisely. Do not be concerned, Mr. Sterling, they are asleep. Besides, bats are our friends. Each night they devour thousands of insects that would otherwise be most troublesome to us."

"I don't care what they eat," I said. "I still hate bats. Yuck!" I guess I spoke too loudly. My echo bounced around the archway like an invisible rubber ball. *Yuck. Uck. Uck.*

"Bats are much less dangerous than some people," Nabi said. Suddenly he had a stern expression on his face, and at first I thought he might be mad at me for what I said about his creepy flying friends. Then I realized he wasn't looking at me. He was squinting and staring over my head. I turned and saw, standing a few yards outside the stone archway, two men I hadn't noticed before. One of them wore an orange djellabah with the hood up, concealing his face. The other man wore a brownish suit. I think it was Ota Sato.

"Our van leaves in half an hour," Babette said. "Shall we look around a bit?"

I glanced at my watch. "Uncle Stoppard, it's almost twelve o'clock."

"Great!" he said. "That will give me time to look for Brentano. Now let's see, if we do this in an organized fashion, then—theoretically, of course—we should be able to see every tomb."

Every tomb!

"Lead on, Señora Lizardo," Abou said.

"It's *señorita*," Babette said, smiling. She put her arm through Abou's and led him off among the ruins.

The Mallomar Tombs were gigantic when you stood right next to them, although some of the spaces in between them were no wider than my bedroom door back home. The five of us had to walk through one passageway single file for a full two minutes before we came to the end of it. After ten more minutes, all the tombs started looking the same to me. Uncle Stoppard kept saying, "A few more yards. I think I hear Brent's voice coming from behind that wall." But we never met another person in the passageways. Not that stranger in the orange djellabah nor the guy in the brownish suit. Where did they go?

It was hard to keep track of everyone among all the alleys and tunnels and staircases and doorways. I felt like a mouse in a laboratory maze. Babette ran up some steps to get a closer look at a weird carving. Abou vanished behind some pillars. Nabi and Uncle Stoppard, still chatting, drifted down a side passageway and would have disappeared if I hadn't whistled at them.

What's so fascinating about a bunch of ruins? Boring hunks of stone.

Except for the knots. That's what Abou said they were called. The Mallomars, according to Abou, loved all kinds of puzzles. They decorated the outer walls of their tombs with colored bits of stone in patterns designed to look like mazes. The most complicated maze-decorations were called knots. Occan tradition said you were supposed to place your finger at one end of the knot, trace the path around and around, looping back and forth as if you were reading an incredibly long sentence in Braille, and finally reach the other end, without lifting your finger, where a prayer in Arabic was carved into the wall.

It took me ten minutes to finish the first one. Then I got the hang of it. The next three went a lot quicker.

"See, Uncle Stop—?"

Where was Uncle Stoppard? Abou, Nabi, and Babette were also missing. Great! Without me to help him,

Uncle Stoppard was sure to get lost. This was like his forgetting to pack back in Minneapolis. We'd miss the ride to Aznac, and the Ruby Raven ceremony.

I had to find him.

As I walked farther into the heart of the great cemetery, the tombs grew higher and wider. The passages stretched out longer and narrower, like earthworms. Some dusty footprints led me into an alley no more than a yard wide. Soon my shoulders were rubbing against the damp walls. A dim ribbon of blue sky high overhead was the only light. I could barely see my shoes.

"Uncle Stop!" I yelled.

Uncle Stoppard's voice came from somewhere beyond the high, damp walls. He sounded as if he were deep under water.

A narrow rectangle of dim, pink light gleamed at me from the end of a long alley. Footsteps. Someone was running, but the sound came from above. Above? I heard a rumbling sound, like a bowling ball rolling across the floor. A *big* bowling ball. An incredible crash shook the alley. The ball must have hit all ten pins.

I ran down the skinny passageway, scraping my arms against the walls. When I reached the end, I discovered that the pink rectangle I had seen was merely light reflecting off a reddish granite wall facing the passage. The noon sunlight felt warm on the top of my head. When I brushed the grit and dust off my arms, my hands came away covered in blood. The ancient Mallomar walls were rougher than I realized.

At the red granite wall, the passageway turned sharply to the right. But I couldn't go on. A huge stone pillar and a cloud of settling dust blocked my way. The pillar was ten times fatter than the trunk of the fallen palm tree, and probably a hundred times heavier.

Footsteps again. Running somewhere far above the

passageway. I didn't know who it was, but this time I knew who it wasn't.

It wasn't Nabi Neez.

From underneath the fallen pillar stuck out a pair of thin legs ending in blue tennis shoes.

Abou appeared, hatless and coatless, behind me. Uncle Stoppard and Babette were yelling from somewhere on the other side of the fallen pillar. The next thing I remember is sitting on the hot leather passenger seat of the canary yellow sports car with my brain spinning and my head in my hands.

"What about the blood?" someone said.

"Don't worry about it," came Abou's voice.

The drive back to Fuz was a blur. When we returned to the Hôtel Splendide, the other writers had reassembled in the jungle lobby. Mr. Hyde stood with his clipboard at his side, his eyes darting back and forth, as usual. "Has anyone seen Mr. Neez or Mr. Zamboni?" he crackled.

Mona noticed the look on Uncle Stoppard's face. "What happened?" she said.

Babette Lizardo, sniffing but dry-eyed, related the accident at the Mallomar Tombs. Everyone was shocked at the news of Nabi Neez's death. Uncle Stoppard explained that the Fuz police had arrived quickly on the scene (Abou had a phone in his car) just as we were leaving.

"I'm sure there will be an autopsy," said Uncle Stoppard.

How could the police perform an autopsy on a pancake? Maybe those blue tennis shoes would tell them something.

"It was dreadful," Babette said. "Why did we ever go to that awful place?"

"You look like you've been working out," Mona said. "Exercising lately?"

Babette stopped sniffing. "What's that supposed to mean?"

"Physics, Babette. With a little leverage, anyone could have pried a heavy pillar down on Neez. Including you."

"That's outrageous!" Babette boomed.

"The nominee list got suddenly smaller," said Mona. "We have the tardy Mr. Zamboni and the late Mr. Neez. Looks like the odds just got better."

"Odds?" Uncle Stoppard said.

Mona looked around at the other writers. Then she drew a puff from her cigarette. "Explain it to them, Hyde."

The little blond man in the pale blue suit did not look as though he enjoyed being ordered around. "What Miss Squeer is referring to—"

"That's Trafalgar-Squeer."

"Ahem. What she is referring to is—"

Mona jumped in. "The fewer writers that end up at the award ceremony"—puff—"the more moolah each person gets."

"Moolah?" said Mr. Hyde.

"Only one person gets the prize," Omar Bah said. "Only one! And that's the winner."

"Yes, the winner gets a million dollars," Mona said. "But another million, a *second* million, is split equally among the losers."

"What?" said everyone else.

"Isn't that right, Hyde?" said Mona.

"Correct," said Mr. Hyde. "The losers, er, other nominees, do indeed receive cash consolation prizes."

"Nice consolation," Abou whispered to me.

"But remember," Mona said. "As the telegram stated, You must be present to win. The losers that share the second million"—puff—"must be at the ceremony. And"—puff—"breathing."

Abou turned to my uncle and said quietly, "Two writers will now be missing from the award ceremony, Zamboni and Neez. That increases each remaining loser's, er, defeatee's portion by forty percent."

"Wow! Everyone's richer," I said.

Abou nodded grimly. "And if the explosion from the mail bomb had been successful, Mr. Sterling, the other nominees would be seventy-five percent richer."

And if the falling palm tree had struck humans, instead of furniture, who knows who would still be standing?

An ice cube was melting at the bottom of my stomach. If I hadn't gone to the library with Uncle Stoppard and dropped that stupid history book on his foot, then he would never have gotten the idea to write about Hamlet. And if he had never written *Into My Grave*, then he'd never have been nominated for the Ruby Raven. And if he hadn't been nominated, then we wouldn't be in some weird country with people throwing bombs and trees at each other. This was all my fault. I made a decision then and there, while standing in the marble lobby of the Le Fuz Hôtel Splendide, and it wasn't an easy decision: I would never visit another library as long as I lived.

Mr. Hyde made a few more announcements. Despite Nabi Neez's tragic death, the ceremony would continue. We all observed a minute of silence in Nabi's memory. I bowed my head and gazed at my copy of *The Case of the Cairo Gyro* still in my hands. In the shiny depths of the marble floor were reflected the bowed heads of the mystery writers. Something bothered me. Something was missing. Mr. Hyde then cleared his throat and pointed out that although Brentano Zamboni was absent, according to the rules of the Nevermore Society, the ceremony could not wait for him, and we should continue on to Aznac.

"Your bus is waiting outside," My. Hyde said, "and will depart in twenty minutes."

"Why Aznac?" I asked Uncle Stoppard.

"It's Poe," said Mona. "The Nevermore Society meets in a different spot each year, but it's always someplace mentioned in the works of Edgar Allan Poe. You know, the fellow who invented the detective story."

I knew who Poe was.

"This year, since Ravenwood moved to Aznac," said Mona, "he decided to have the ceremony in Occo."

"I don't remember a Poe story about Aznac," Abou said.

"It's the one with the mummy," Mr. Hyde said. "Let's get on board, everyone."

Babette bounded over and put her arm through Abou's. "Will you be joining us, Mr. Abou?"

Abou glanced at Uncle Stoppard and me, and then back at Babette. "Yes, indeed, Miss Lizardo. I'm covering the story for *Peephole* magazine, you know."

"Photographs, too?" asked Babette.

I watched Babette and Abou stroll toward the revolving front door of the hotel. Mr. ben Wittgenstein was wrong: three writers were missing, not two. Nada Kloo, listed right after Omar Bah, was ignored by the spooky Mr. Hyde. Where was she? And something else was missing. Something at the edge of my memory, off the top of my head. I looked over at Uncle Stoppard, who was pulling Mona aside on her way out. "You don't believe Nabi Neez's death was an accident," he said. "You truly believe that somebody pushed that pillar?"

Mona flicked the butt of her cigarette into a nearby palm pot. "All I'm saying, Stoppard, is that we better watch our heads."

5
The Mummy

"Beware his chimpanzees," Babette whispered to me. "Mr. Wittgenstein is a sly one."

During the bus trek to Truman Ravenwood's mansion in Aznac, Uncle Stoppard and the other writers discussed the death of Nabi Neez and argued about mystery stories. At one point I heard Uncle Stoppard say, *"Shakespeare* was never afraid to use clichés." Mona said, "And heaven knows, you aren't either." Abou and Babette were teaching me to play chess with a small traveling chessboard of Abou's. The chess pieces had magnets inside that kept them from sliding off the metal game board whenever the bus hit a bump. Each piece was a different African animal: the king and queen were lions, the knights were zebras, the pawns were chimpanzees. We played for hours, as the landscape outside the bus windows changed from Fuz to forest to mountain to rocky plain. Babette gave me some good tips.

"Watch his pawns," she whispered over my shoulder, during one of my turns with Abou. "People forget that little pawns can be important pieces. We have a saying back in Barcelona: When the game is over, the king and the pawn are put in the same box."

The mystery bus was sleek and modern and roomy, with air-conditioning and tinted windows. Our driver was a shy Occan named Muhammad. When we boarded the bus outside the hotel, he avoided looking at our eyes, out of respect, when he spoke with us, but he kept a good eye on the road. Abou said that Occans were an extremely polite people. They followed lots of complicated rules and manners to avoid offending anyone. "Occans are especially hospitable to guests," said Abou. Every so often, I would look up from the chessboard and glance out the windows. I noticed that many of the road signs were printed in three languages: English, Arabic, and Japanese. Somehow, bombing Japanese people did not seem hospitable to me.

Abou, Babette, and I sat near the back of the bus. Uncle Stoppard, Mona, Omar Bah, and Ota Sato sat toward the front. Each of us had our own seat. Mr. Hyde, the blond marionette, did not ride with us. He stayed at the hotel to "tie up loose ends," he said, and wait for the unfortunate Mr. Zamboni. He would join us later in Aznac by private helicopter.

"All right, Mona," said Uncle Stoppard. "Now you try them on."

"I am not trying them on," she said.

Ota Sato had brought a pair of Japanese handcuffs with him. It was for his next book, he said. He was trying to see if a person could escape from the cuffs without using a key. He had worked with them by himself for two months, but without success, and was hoping one of the other writers could make like Houdini and slip out of the wicked-looking shackles. If not, Sato would have to go back and delete six whole chapters! I remembered Uncle Stoppard doing research on one of his own mysteries and trying to haul himself up the side of our apartment building using only a fishing pole. He landed in a lilac bush and then the hospital.

Omar Bah was fiddling with the cuffs as our bus drove alongside a wide lake in the middle of a flat

purple plain. The lake was pink, pinker than our bedroom in the Hôtel Splendide. Flamingos, thousands of
them, waded and skittered across the surface of the
water. As if on cue, all the flamingos leaped into the
air, swirled together into a pink cyclone, and then flew
over the bus, blocking the sunlight for more than a
minute.

Abou talked about his life while moving his zebras
and chimpanzees around the chessboard. He had
traveled all over the world with his mother, the
princess—Hong Kong, Singapore, India, Australia,
Italy, Spain. He said his next trip would be to a cold
country.

"We're going to Iceland next," I said. "If Uncle Stoppard wins the Raven."

"If he doesn't win the Raven," said Babette, "He will
not come away empty-handed."

"Yes," said Abou. "Remember the consolation prizes."

Throughout the long ride to Aznac, Babette scribbled
in a purple notebook. She said Abou would make an interesting character for her next book.

"Will I be the hero or the killer?" Abou asked.

Babette smiled mysteriously. "Whoever you are," she
said, "you'll be crashing a grave."

"Crashing a grave?" Abou said.

"Dashing and brave," repeated Babette.

It was hard to hear one another. Huge orange-brown
clouds blotted out the sun. Where was that lake? Ahead
of us lay a dark wall of churning smoke.

"A sandstorm," said Abou, quietly. "A bad one."

"Shouldn't Muhammad turn us around?" I said.

"We are four hours from Fuz," he said. "The best
thing is to stay put, or keep driving forward."

Darkness engulfed the bus. Muhammad switched on
his windshield wipers and headlights. The roaring of the

storm outside grew louder than the bus's engine or air-conditioner.

"This storm"—puff—"has been going on"—puff—"for days!"

"It's been twenty minutes, Mona," Uncle Stoppard said.

Sand blew through tiny chinks in the windows. Many of the writers were holding scarves or hankies over their mouths. Mona kept smoking. "How long"—puff—"do you think this"—puff—"storm will last?"

"Storms like these," Omar Bah said, "have been known to last for hours."

"Four hours!" Mona gasped.

"Four hours!" gasped Muhammad. At least, that's what I think he said. It was hard to hear with the wind whistling and roaring and making more noise than a closet full of cats. Muhammad, I could tell, was scared. He was steering directly into the storm. The windshield resembled an ant farm.

"This is fantastic!" Babette exclaimed.

"Being suffocated is fantastic?" Mona said. If she put out that little black cigarette, maybe she could breath.

"No," Babette said. "I mean a tour bus stranded in the middle of a desert during a raging sandstorm."

"I was caught in an Australian sandstorm once," said Abou.

"And such an exotic name," said Babette. "The *Grand Occidental Erg.*"

"Erg?" said Mona. "Where's that?"

"This is it, darling," said Babette. "We are in the *erg.*"

Uncle Stoppard coughed up some sand. "It seems the *erg* is in us, as well."

"An *erg,*" Abou shouted to me, "is a vast sandy area of the Sahara."

"That is the French word," Omar Bah said. "We call it an *irk.*"

Moving walls of sand shuddered along the sides of the bus.

"I call it irking," said Mona.

"What's the matter, Mona?" Babette asked.

"I hadn't planned on being in the middle of a disaster movie, that's all!"

"I thought you were the queen of death and dying."

"On the printed page, yes," Mona said. "Not on some lousy back road in some"—puff—"jerkwater Third World country."

Omar Bah made a snorting sound. A loud snorting sound. Not the kind of snorting sound we were all making as the sand blizzard grew fiercer, sifting through the seams along the windows, stinging our eyes and throats. It was more like the sound a particularly large bull makes before it charges and tramples a weak, defenseless creature in its path.

"Third World?" he bellowed. "Jerk your water?"

I had never seen Mona speechless before. Omar Bah rose from his seat. His shoulders towered like the Atlas Mountains. His magnificent mustache quivered like a condor flapping its wings.

In other words, as they say in the *erg,* the camel dung was about to hit the fan. I was looking forward to the battle royal between the Queen of Crime and the Bull of Occo. I never got the chance. At that moment the bus decided to tip over.

A grinding crash of metal and rubber. Omar Bah was no longer standing. He was lying on the side of the bus, along with the rest of us, buried beneath an *erg* of luggage and bodies. The right side of the bus was now the floor, and the floor and ceiling were now vertical. I felt I was inside a clothes dryer after it shut off.

Mona was no longer smoking. Smoldering maybe, but not smoking. I knew that because my right knee was in her mouth. Uncle Stoppard lay sprawled over the groaning Babette. I could see one of her braceleted hands, fat fingers still clutching her pencil, sticking out from behind Uncle Stoppard's white shirt. Ota Sato was digging Muhammad out from beneath a small mountain of costume jewelry, wigs, makeup and shoes. It probably belonged to Babette, since most of the luggage was hers. Three enormous pink leather suitcases with B.L. stamped in gold were lying on Abou. One of his two-toned shoes poked out from the Lizardo luggage. His other foot, shoeless, wore a brown and orange argyle sock decorated with little red bats.

"Is everyone all right?" Ota Sato yelled.

Mona shouted, "Are you trying to win the Stupid Question contest? Of course, we're not all right. That idiot driver! Who's foot is that?"

"I think it's mine," Uncle Stoppard said. "Are those my glasses?"

"The driver must be blind," Mona said.

"I believe I'm wearing your glasses," said Babette.

"Does anyone have a light? A flashlight?" Mona asked.

The storm clouds, which could be glimpsed through the shattered windows, now above our heads, turned from orange-brown to brownish red.

"I think there's a torch in the glove compartment," Abou said.

"What exactly happened?" Ota Sato asked.

"We tipped over," I said.

"There was a woman," said Muhammad.

We all turned to look at our driver.

"A woman?" Babette asked.

Muhammad nodded, nervously. "All in white. With

her arms like this." He raised his hands above his tur-
ban. "I didn't want to hit her, so I turned the wheel."

"You're seeing things," Mona said.

"Yes," said Muhammad. "I am seeing a woman."

"No," Omar Bah said. "Not a woman."

Bah had finally pulled himself out from the clothes
heap and was sitting on Uncle Stoppard's duffel bag.
His voice had a spooky, hollow tone to it. I think that's
why we all stared at him.

"It was not a woman," he repeated. "It was a ghoul."
Omar Bah's mustache wings, tilted at different angles,
stuck out from the sides of a white handkerchief he held
over his mouth to keep out the sand. How could sand
penetrate that thick hedge of a beard?

"A ghoul?" said Uncle Stoppard.

"An hour ago," Omar Bah said, "we passed through a
cleft in the rocks known as Bab el-Ghul, the Gate of the
Ghoul."

Like the archway to the Mallomar tombs.

"We are in strange country now," Bah said.

Babette licked her lips. "Is the ghoul a male or a female, Mr. Bah?"

"Neither. A ghoul is a blood-drinking demon that
takes the shape of a human, usually a woman."

I wondered if a ghoul could smoke cigarettes and
write prize-winning mysteries.

"The ghoul deceives its victims," Omar Bah said, "in
order to get close enough to attack."

"Like the *tanaghout*," Abou said.

Omar Bah regarded Abou with a curious stare, as if
he were seeing him for the first time. "And you are—?"

"Abou ben Wittgenstein. From the Occan branch of
Peephole magazine."

Bah's mustache ends twitched. "Wittgenstein is not
an Occan name."

"My father's Max Wittgenstein, the publisher," said Abou.

"Occan men are raised to respect their elders and keep silent."

"How do you spell tana—whatzit?" Babette asked. She had found her purple notebook and was jotting notes again.

"The *tanaghout*," said Abou, "is a poisonous desert snake that bleats like a goat to lure other goats to their deaths. That's what some people believe, anyway."

"True Occans believe," said Omar Bah, "that ghouls are actually the spirits of the former desert gods. When Muhammad the Prophet—peace be with him!—entered Mecca in 630 A.D. and destroyed the idols, the angry spirits, which had lived inside the idols for centuries, went forth in search of souls."

A blast of wind shivered the bus.

"Perhaps it is ancient al-Uzzah we hear, howling for blood," Omar Bah said. "Or blind Qa'is, or Nuhm, the goddess of lost roads."

High above the howling of the wind, I heard a bright and haunting sound. A woman's cry pierced the storm.

Babette grabbed my uncle's arm. Mona turned green.

Another cry. "It's getting closer," Mona said.

"Look," Omar Bah said.

"Look," echoed Muhammad, pointing through the cracked windshield. "Out there."

Slowly, eerily, through the dark-orange swirling sands emerged a figure. Long, skinny, white arms, claw-like hands, a flowing white fabric wrapped around its head.

"The Mummy of Aznac," said Ota Sato.

The figure reached out toward the bus.

This can't be happening. Mummies aren't real. Another unearthly cry pierced the storm, **and** the back of my neck turned to ice.

"It's shouting in English!" shouted Abou.

Muhammad scurried away from the windshield as the white figure approached. The mummy bent down and glared at us through its veil of bandages, its ghostly face mere inches from the glass. It reminded me of the cobra back at the Hôtel Splendide, staring at me through the glass door of the shower stall. A white cobra, ready to strike. Bony white hands banged against the windshield. How strong was this creature?

"Well, of course I spoke in English!" said the mummy. "You wouldn't answer when I tried French. Now help me out of this wind or I'll die out here!"

6
Devil's Desert

If—and that was a big if—we had wanted to let the creature inside, there was no easy way. The windows on the left side of the bus were now resting on the ground. The windshield, though cracked, was still solid. And the other row of windows, along with the door of the bus, was above our heads, keeping out the billowing gusts of sand and dust.

The mummy scrambled up the slanting hood of the bus and crouched by the spinning front right tire. Then the white figure climbed up onto the bus's side, which was now the roof. White fists pounded against the door.

"Who are you?" I shouted.

The creature crawled across the door and onto one of the windows. Without warning, the half-broken window popped open, swinging inward on its hinges, and the creature toppled into the bus. It was like slow motion. The mummy's bandages—or robe, I guess it was— caught on the window frame, so for a second I caught a glimpse of dangling legs and funny blue underwear. Mummies wear underwear? Fruit of the Tomb? There was a horrible ripping sound, the robe pulled free, and the creature was among us.

"I thought you wouldn't stop," said the mummy, adjusting the gloves over its claw-like hands. The creature sat propped up on a heap of clothes. It bent its veiled face to look down at us. "I imagined myself wandering the desert like Moses and the Israelites, while the Ruby Raven went to someone else. Probably to that dreadful Mona person."

"Get off me!"

Who said that?

"That sounded exactly like Trafalgar-Squeer," said the mummy.

"That's because it *is* me!"

The mummy lifted its robe. The heap of clothes it was sitting on turned out to be Mona, red-faced and snarling.

"Who are you?" Uncle Stoppard asked.

Ota Sato extended his right hand toward the creature. "It is Nada Kloo, our fellow nominee from Russia."

A white claw grabbed the hand of the bespectacled ex–sumo wrestler. I could see now that the mummy was indeed a woman, wearing a long white jacket and skirt beneath a flowing white robe. She also wore a white hat, white gloves and a thick veil that completely hid her face from view. "How kind of you to remember me, Sato-san, from the murder convention in Tokyo."

"Where did you come from?" I asked.

The bus lurched. A loud grinding shuddered upward through our feet.

"We must hurry," said Nada Kloo. "I was trying to warn you, this road has a cliff to one side. And the wind is blowing in that direction."

"We better find shelter," said Omar Bah.

Nada Kloo held up her gloved hands. "Wait. Before we go looking for shelter we must first find Alexy."

"Who?" Babette asked.

"My pilot," Kloo said.

"You flew here?" said Abou.

"Alexander insisted on taking us in his own plane; he

got his pilot's license last month, you see. We left Nice at dawn and had breakfast in Barcelona, with plenty of time to reach Fuz. But the Occan authorities would not let us land. Said something about bomb threats. Can you believe it? They said we'd have to circle before landing, maybe for an hour! There was no way I was going to—"

Another grinding sound as the bus scraped along the ground.

"We arrived in Fuz minutes after your bus left," said Nada. "Did you know there's a murder investigation at the hotel?"

"Yes," said Ota Sato. "Mr. Neez of Egypt."

"Not him," Kloo said. "Though I heard all about him. No, this was someone else. The hotel manager was quite upset. Two deaths connected with the hotel all in one day."

"Who was the other?" Babette asked.

A strong gust of wind shoved us a few more inches along the ground.

"We must hurry," said Omar Bah. "Miss Kloo can finish her story once we have found a safe place out of this storm."

Uncle Stoppard unfolded a map of Occo he carried in his belt pack. "Mr. Sato, hand that torch, er, flashlight over here. Let's see. Here's Bab el-Ghul, which we passed about forty minutes ago. Muhammad, what was your average speed during the storm?"

Muhammad shrugged. "Maybe twenty kilometers per hour, sir."

"That's less than fifteen miles per hour," Uncle Stoppard said.

"Twelve point six," Abou said.

"Thanks, Abou. So, we should be right about there." Uncle Stoppard pointed to a spot on the map.

Kloo grabbed the map and peered at it through her veil. "The *Eagle*—that's the name of Alexie's three-seater—was traveling south-southeast toward Aznac. I could see your bus on our port side before we hit the storm. Over there." She jabbed at the map. "To the right of the highway. I could see pink buildings. Alexy saw them, too. We landed about two hundred yards away from them. Then the wind got much worse. We waited for the storm to clear, but it seemed like it would never stop, and Alexy was worried that the wind would blow us farther away from the village. So we got out of the plane and that's when we became separated."

"How long have you been walking?" Uncle Stop asked.

Kloo glanced down at a watch she wore on a chain around her neck. "Fifteen minutes, I think, before I saw the light from your headlamps."

"The plane couldn't be more than half a mile from here," Abou said.

"And the village can't be much farther," Ota Sato said.

"What about Alexy?" Kloo cried.

Uncle Stoppard looked up from the map. "Alexy could have made it to the village by now. Does anyone have a compass?"

Abou pulled a small silver disk from the inside of his yellow jacket. Kloo snatched it before he could hand it to Uncle Stoppard.

"South-southeast," she said, examining the instrument. "And the bus was traveling due east. Ah, we need to go in that direction."

"But it's getting dark," Mona said.

"It will get much darker," Omar Bah said. "And much colder. I suggest we each take only what we can carry and head for the village."

"But there's no village showing on the map," I said to Uncle Stoppard.

"That's got me worried, too," he said. "But sometimes tiny villages aren't marked."

After lots of pulling and shoving, and lots of what Uncle Stoppard calls "blue language" contributed by Mona, we finally stood outside the bus. We looked like survivors from a shipwreck. Without our added weight, the bus moved several more feet toward a yawning darkness that I guessed was the edge of the cliff.

"Join hands," yelled Kloo.

I was glad Uncle Stoppard had bought those djellabahs back at the airport. We each slipped one on and pulled the hoods down over our faces. Kloo headed the line. It was easy for her since she had no luggage to carry, it was all in the *Eagle*. With her left hand she held the compass inside her veil. Her skinny right hand held on to Omar Bah. Bah's other hand joined Babette's. Next came Abou (still missing one shoe), Uncle Stoppard and me, and then Mona, Ota Sato, and Muhammad. Babette talked Muhammed into carrying one of her suitcases since he had no luggage but did have a free hand.

Who was this faceless Nada Kloo? Her veil was certainly useful. Was she always prepared in case of sandstorms? Or was there another reason she wore it? There was something she had said when we were inside the bus, something that didn't make sense. At the time, I thought how it was something that she shouldn't have had to say. What was it? The wind seemed to have blown it out of my brain.

"Close your eyes if you must," Kloo shouted. "My veil keeps the sand out of my face, so I'll lead."

"The blind leading the blind," Mona yelled back..

*   *   *

The Arabs are famous for making nothing. I mean Nothing. Zero. According to Uncle Stoppard, the zero, or cipher as he calls it, was their greatest invention. Where would a million bucks be without the zeros? In fact, the word *cipher* comes from the same word that the name Sahara comes from: *zifr*. People living in the Grand Occidental Erg or other parts of the Desert call their home the Great Nothing. The Void. The Big Empty Space.

Now I know why.

After we left the bus and played follow-the-leader through the sandstorm, it felt like we were nowhere. East Nowhere. Nine figures lost inside a giant zero. I couldn't see anything, smell anything, or taste anything, except sand. All I could hear was the growling of the storm. Sometimes, and I know this sounds weird, sometimes I could hear voices in the wind. People singing, or crying, or laughing at me. Was that the storm or my ears ringing? I couldn't tell. Only when someone in line shouted or coughed did the normal sounds of the storm return. My two unchanging grips with reality were the pull of Uncle Stoppard's hand on my left, and the drag of Mona Trafalgar-Squeer's on my right. She needed to trim her fingernails.

The dim light pressing on my tightly shut eyelids grew dimmer. Sometimes the light went out completely, probably from a thickening wave of dust. At those times, Uncle Stoppard's hand gripped me tighter.

"How can Nada Kloo read the compass without a light?" I yelled.

"It's luminous," Uncle Stoppard shouted.

Luminous? Oh, right, those tiny blobs of green stuff that glow in the dark.

I was worried that we might end up wandering around for days. No, someone will come looking for us.

They've got to. The Nevermore Society must know about the storm. Mr. Hyde will send out a search party. They'll find the bus and— Wait. What if it blows for days? And what if Mr. Hyde's helicopter was also caught in the sandstorm, like Kloo and her friend's plane?

A thousand burning needles stabbed the arches of my feet. I felt sorry for one-shoe Abou. It's not easy walking for miles and miles on soft sand and hard rock.

Kloo shouted. Uncle Stoppard stopped pulling with his hand. The growling of the wind grew fainter. The sand blowing against my cheeks felt weaker. We must be inside the village walls. I opened my eyes.

"This is definitely not a village," Mona said.

We stood inside the mouth of a dark, narrow canyon. Towering rock walls, black as charcoal, pressed in on both sides. The canyon reminded me of that creepy passageway in the Mallomar cemetery where Nabi Neez began his journey to the Farthest Mosque. The black canyon was much wider, though, about twenty feet across. A curtain of smoke and dust hung across the mouth of the canyon, the wind whistled and screamed. I looked at Mona and noticed her neon-blue suit was no longer neon. It wasn't blue, either. Omar Bah's suit had turned from vanilla to chocolate. I gazed down at my striped djellabah; the stripes were gone. Everyone was caked with Sahara dust. All our clothes were the same color: *erg.*

"What is this place?" Babette puffed, nearly out of breath. She had tied a long scarf over her straw hat to keep it from blowing away in the wind, and was now loosening the knot beneath her several chins.

"These are the Teeth of Darkness," Omar Bah said.

"Whose teeth?" I said.

"An immense rock formation of red and black sandstone," Bah said, "that stretches between the Fuzi mountains and Aznac. Parts of it have never been explored."

After Bah's comment, I noticed deep red veins running through the black cliffs.

"Doesn't anything in this country have a pleasant-sounding name?" Mona said.

"I followed the compass correctly," Kloo said. "Look." She showed the compass to Abou. "Doesn't the arrow show south-southeast is this direction?"

"Well, yes," Abou said slowly. "But it shows north in every other direction."

"What?" Mona shouted.

"The needle is stuck," Abou said.

"From all the sand," Babette groaned. She lowered herself wearily onto a large, red rock.

Kloo held her watch to her ear. "This wretched watch has stopped, too. I hadn't noticed before. Now I can't be sure how long I was wandering before I saw the bus."

Abou tapped his digital. "It's seven thirty-two," he said. The sun would set in about an hour.

"That's terrific," Mona said. "Couldn't you tell the compass was broken when the arrow refused to move?"

"I thought I was traveling in a straight line," Kloo said. "My sense of direction is extremely reliable."

Uncle Stoppard pulled out his map from beneath his robe, while Abou held the flashlight over Uncle Stop's shoulder. Everyone crowded around the wrinkled map.

"The Teeth of Darkness are here," said Uncle Stoppard. "North-northwest of the highway to Aznac. We've been traveling in the opposite direction."

"Alexy!" Kloo wailed.

Mona pulled a cigarette from her purse and lit it. "What next?" she asked.

"At least we're out of the storm," Uncle Stoppard said. "Maybe we'll have better luck finding the village in the morning."

"You intend to stay here"—puff—"overnight?"

"You have a better idea?"

"The award ceremony is tonight," Mona said. "I have to be present to collect my million."

"*Your* million?" Babette said. "What if it's *my* million?"

"This year," Kloo said, "the Ruby Raven flies home to Mother Russia."

"Perhaps the Raven flies over Mother Russia to rest in Japan," said Ota Sato.

"That Bird is not leaving this country!" bellowed Bah.

Uncle Stoppard whistled to get everyone's attention. "There won't be any award ceremony tonight, people! All of the candidates are *us*. And all of us are right here."

"Except for Nabi," I said.

"Yes, except for Nabi," said Uncle Stoppard.

"And Brentano," Babette said.

"Where exactly is our pal Zamboni?" Mona asked.

Murdered at the Hôtel Splendide?

"I thought I saw him at the Mallomar tombs," said Uncle Stoppard.

"He told me he was going sightseeing," Babette said. "But if he was up at Mallomar, he never came back."

"You mean, he didn't come back with *you*," Mona said. "What if he had his own transportation back to the hotel? Or to Aznac? I'll bet he hitched a ride with that Hyde character after Nada left the hotel, and now he's sitting pretty with the Raven."

"Maybe he got lost up at Mallomar," Babette said.

"He probably planned this whole thing," Mona said.

"You can't plan a sandstorm, Ms. Squeer," said Ota Sato.

"That's Trafalgar-Squeer. Okay, maybe he didn't plan the storm. But he could have paid old Wrong-Way Muhammad here to get us lost."

Muhammad may not have understood everything being said about him, but he could tell when people were staring at him.

"By Allah, I am a good driver," Muhammad cried.

"How much is Zamboni paying you?" Mona said.

"Don't be stupid, Mona," said Uncle Stoppard.

"Keep out of this, Sterling."

Everyone started talking at once. Muhammad sat down on Babette's suitcase and put his head in his hands. "Zamboni didn't hire Muhammad," I said. "Mr. Hyde arranged the transportation to Aznac."

"Yes, yes," said Muhammad, nodding at me. "Mr. Hyde."

"What shall we do about Alexy?" Nada wailed.

"There is only one road between Fuz and Aznac," said Uncle Stoppard. "There is no other route we could have traveled."

Mona lit another cigarette. "Maybe Zamboni hired Muhammad to fake an accident."

"There are no accidents," said Omar Bah, squinting at her through his tiny gold glasses.

Mona grunted. "Is that another colorful tidbit of Occan folklore we're supposed to believe in, like ghouls and monsters?"

"Who is that?" shouted Babette. She pointed at the billowing curtain of smoke and dust that bordered the entrance of the canyon.

I didn't see anyone. Only dust.

"I saw a man," Babette said. "There's a man out there!"

Goosebumps ran up and down my arms. Another mummy? A real one, this time?

"Alexy!" cried Kloo.

We waited, but no one stepped out of the storm.

"I'm going out there," Kloo said.

"Wait," said Omar Bah. "It could have been an illusion. Many travelers caught in sandstorms tell of seeing figures and shapes in the wind. Whole armies have been seen, marching into battle."

Did those same travelers hear phantoms singing and laughing?

"It's too dangerous to go back out there, Miss Kloo," said Uncle Stoppard.

Mona turned to Babette. "You're seeing things."

"Am I? Like Muhammad was 'seeing things' when he saw Nada? She turned out to be real, didn't she?" Babette began to angrily shake the dust from her long skirt.

Above the canyon rim, the clouds were boiling pink. The sun was setting. The steep red walls turned to blood. Nada Kloo was a scarlet mummy. The tip of Mona's cigarette burned like an orange star in the deepening gloom. Where was Abou?

"Hey!" Abou's voice. "Come quickly."

Abou had wandered about fifty feet farther into the canyon. "Look," he said, pointing his flashlight to either side. Iron doors, ancient with rust, hung inward on massive hinges. The doors formed the only entrance through a giant iron gate spanning the whole width of the narrow canyon.

"Shine your light up there," said Uncle Stoppard. "I think there's some writing."

Across the top of the silent doorway, Abou's light dis-

covered an iron plaque engraved with harsh-looking letters. The letters were not Arabic.

Mortville

"Death City," Kloo whispered.
"Is this a village?" I asked.
"Not a village," Omar Bah said.

Abou elbowed his way to the front of the group. "I
don't believe it," he said, staring up at the sign. He ran
through the doorway and disappeared behind a rocky
bend in the passage.

I ran after him.

7
City of Death

Abou waved his flashlight back and forth. A man with one arm. A bull with lowered horns. A wide flight of steps, carved from the same red stone as the two statues, led up to a forest of rose-colored pillars.

"A Roman temple," Babette said.

"It must be centuries old," said Uncle Stoppard.

The canyon was seriously dark. We could see only what the flashlight beam picked out, towering pillars and doorways and lots of stairs. It reminded me of our old library back home.

"Why would a Roman temple," Mona said, "if it is a Roman temple, have a French name?"

Good question. And why Mortville, the city of death?

"Mr. ben Wittgenstein," Omar Bah said. "Do you know your ancient history?"

Abou took off his one remaining shoe and stood stocking-footed in the sand. "I know the Romans invaded Occo in the third century B.C.," he said.

Omar Bah stared disapprovingly at Abou's dusty brown and orange socks. "Occo has suffered under many invaders," Bah said. "The Romans, the Vandals, the Turks . . . the Japanese." (Mr. Sato remained silent.) "The Germans in World War Two. And before that, the French."

"The Foreign Legion," Abou said.

Omar Bah's massive black beard bobbed up and down on his chest. His tiny spectacles glittered in the reflected flashlight beam. "Mortville was their most notorious outpost. A prison. Nicknamed the Devil's Desert."

"I've read about that," Babette said. "France's most dangerous criminals were sent here and imprisoned for life."

"There was no escape from Mortville," Bah said. "The desert stretched a hundred kilometers in all directions."

"Before the highway got here," Mona pointed out.

Omar Bah squared his shoulders. "The prison was built in the 1830s, on the foundations of a Roman fortress. That is why you see pillars and statues alongside modern metal doors." He marched up the stone steps. "And something far deadlier, if I'm not mistaken. Wittgenstein, bring your torch."

"Too bad they didn't mention this in the travel brochure," Mona said, climbing up after Omar Bah.

Past the forest of pillars, a black square entrance yawned before us. Our footsteps echoed. We must have been walking through a large hallway. It was hard to judge distances in that darkness, but somewhere ahead of us yawned another square, not as black as the first. Did the hallway lead back outside? No, there was no sound of the storm.

"Wow!" I said.

"It's gigantic," said Uncle Stoppard.

"And there she is," pointed Omar Bah.

Sandstorms cover miles and miles of ground, but they're not deep. The air gets clearer about a hundred feet up. That's what I'm guessing, anyway, because of what we saw. We wouldn't have seen it, period, if the Occan sky above Mortville hadn't been partially clear of sand clouds, allowing the sun's last red gleams to burn along the upper edges of the Teeth of Darkness. The hallway ended abruptly in a wide stone landing and a second series of steps leading back down. The steps led to the dusty red floor of a huge, circular arena. Uncle Stoppard called it "vast." The high walls of the arena were lined with hundreds of dark, rectangular mouths. Each mouth was a metal door. Four rows of metal doors lined the curving walls. The first row ran along the sandy floor. The other three rows were reached by separate stone walkways, three big balconies that circled the yard. I noticed two flights of worn steps, one on either side of us, that filed upward from the landing on which we stood.

"Prison cells," said Abou.

But that's not what Omar Bah was pointing to. In the center of the arena, on the sandy floor next to a dark, gaping pit, stood a tall wooden structure. I recognized the evil structure from some old movies on TV. It was a guillotine.

Abou ran down the steps and across the floor of the prison.

"Amazing," Kloo said.

"Did they use that on live human beings?" I asked.

Omar Bah nodded. "The national razor of France, they called it. Used on only the most depraved of criminals."

Abou looked back at us and waved. Standing next to the guillotine, he was tall enough to slip his head into the rounded wooden neck-holder. As a joke he stuck his head through. "I'm King Louis," he laughed. Abou's arm must have struck the guillotine. A glint of metal flashed at the top of the frame. Abou stood up, still laughing. A heavy blade crashed into the neck-holder. Babette screamed. Or was that Uncle Stoppard? Abou leaped back from the evil machine and fell onto the sand.

"It still works!" Mona said.

"Amazing," Kloo said.

Abou was thoughtfully rubbing his neck. I didn't care what Omar Bah had said to Mona back at the entrance to the canyon. Sometimes there *are* accidents. And this accident would have sent Abou's model head, with its perfect teeth and inky black hair, rolling off the wooden guillotine and plopping down into the nearby pit.

Would Abou's eyes have worked as his head rolled over and over? Would his last vision be of the Mortville arena spinning around him? My own neck felt hot. Blood pounded in my head.

What was the dark pit, anyway? Abou must have been wondering the same thing. He crawled over and pointed his flashlight beam into the gaping hole.

"Bones?" Babette called out.

"Fox bones," Abou shouted back. "Looks like a *fanak* fell in and got trapped. But who knows how long ago."

The tips of the Teeth high above the arena were glowing a dim red. Dark shreds of clouds skimmed over the vast circle of the prison yard.

"This place gives me the creeps," Mona said.

"Where are we going to sleep?" I said to Uncle Stoppard.

He glanced around and ran a hand through his spiky red hair. "There must be an officers' quarters nearby," he said. "They probably had beds or cots."

"They might have taken them with them," Ota Sato said.

"They didn't take *that*," Uncle Stoppard said, nodding toward the guillotine. "Maybe the Legionnaires left in a hurry."

The hall behind us was full of creepy statues. Between two red sandstone guys with spears and swords, Uncle Stoppard found a second hallway that led off at a right angle to the main one. Down this smaller hallway, two wooden doors faced each other from opposite walls. A third red guy, this one bald and pointing straight at us, stood on a stone platform at the far end of the hall.

"The emperor Heliogabalus." Abou read the inscription on the base of the statue.

"The mad emperor," Babette said.

"What was he mad about?" I said.

"He was insane mad," said Omar Bah. "He thought God was a big black stone."

Okay, I suppose some people might think that was crazy.

The two wooden doors opened into two big, empty rooms. No windows, no furniture, cool rust-colored floors. This would be like sleeping in a museum. But each room also had a huge fireplace, and an hour later, two warm fires were burning brightly. Ota Sato and Mona, using her lighter as a miniature torch, had discovered old chairs and tables and bits of wood in other rooms of the temple-prison. Babette and I kept the fires going, while the others took turns with the flashlight. Abou and Uncle Stoppard hunted up eight cots. "I won't use one," said Ota Sato. "I usually sleep on the floor. Old sumo school habit."

Omar Bah came back from an expedition loaded down with green-and-red woolen blankets. "Legionnaire colors," he said. "There is also a stable, with straw for bedding." Babette talked Ota into laying down straw for his bed, instead of sleeping directly on the hard sandstone.

It had been hours since the chocolate shake and the Ali Baba burgers at Burger Sheik's. But I was more tired than hungry. The red-and-green blankets looked comfy and warm. Before bedding down, Uncle Stoppard, Abou, Omar Bah, and I walked across the hall to say good night.

"We're not exactly helpless over here," Mona said.

"I was telling Nada about the tragedy back at Mallo-mar," Babette said. "If Nabi hadn't stopped to tie his shoe, you or I might have . . . *Caramba!* I don't want to think about it."

I didn't want to think about Nabi Neez anymore, ei-ther, so I went back to the men's room. I looked through my traveling bag for my toothbrush. Out of the corner of my eye, I watched Uncle Stoppard through the open doorways, in case he needed my help. Omar Bah seemed to be staring across the hall and into our room. What a creepy expression! No wonder he writes mys-teries. I turned back to my suitcase and dug out my toothbrush. Wait, we didn't have any water. I guess we'd have to search for some in the morning. If the Legion-naires lived here, there must have been water nearby, like a pool or a well. But how was I going to brush my teeth tonight? I hate to go to bed with dirty teeth. Soda pop. Maybe someone brought a Coke with them from the bus.

Ota Sato was snoring. Muhammad was standing next to his cot, staring at the fire. When Muhammad noticed me looking at him, he said, "Young man, would you be so kind?"

He slowly, painfully lowered himself onto his cot. "I am sore from the steering wheel," he said, rubbing his chest. He must have slammed into the wheel during the accident. "Could you please remove my shoes for me?"

"No problemo," I said.

I pulled off his left shoe, one of those funny-looking slippers with the curly toes. Too bad I never bought a pair back at the gift shop in the Fuz airport. On the bot-tom of Muhammad's foot was a curious design. It looked like the letter C—the grade I got in Mr. Hud-son's geography class.

"Cool tattoo," I said.

"A birthmark," he said, smiling thinly. "A sign of good fortune. It is shaped like the crescent moon and means that my luck shall be bright as the moon."

I wondered if this was the foot that hit the brake when the bus tipped over.

After I took off his other shoe, Muhammad thanked me, lay down, and pulled one of the ancient blankets over him.

The room was full of warmth and firelight, but no soda pop. I walked back over to the women's room. In between the two bedrooms, in the dark hallway, the two campfires cast weird flickering shadows on the statue and the walls. The bald Roman emperor blinked at me as I walked past him.

I almost rammed into Omar Bah. He marched out through the women's doorway without so much as glancing at me. And the expression on his face! It reminded me of how Nabi had looked when he squinted over my shoulder at the orange stranger under the Mallomar archway. What ever happened to that guy?

Inside the women's room, Babette and Mona were laughing.

"Oh, dear," said Babette. "I hope my little joke didn't offend Mr. Bah."

"I'm sure it wasn't that," Uncle Stoppard said. "I heard him say something about his soul. It's probably prayer time."

Abou glanced at his digital. "Yes, there was no time for the regular afternoon prayer or the sunset prayer," he said. "But we can always make them up later. As long as it is not midnight." Abou bowed. "Ladies, gentlemen, sleep well." Then he stepped into the hall. I figured he was going to join Omar Bah and thank Allah for saving his neck from the guillotine. I'm glad that Uncle Stoppard and I are Christians so that we don't have to pray so much.

"Excuse me, Miss Kloo," said Uncle Stoppard. "But who was killed back at the hotel?"

"Thanks for reminding me," she said. "I had forgotten all about that. But I don't know who it was. The body couldn't be identified. A security guard found it stuffed into one of the urns holding the potted palms."

Uncle Stoppard shot me a glance.

"Do you think," I said, "that it could be Brentano Zamboni?"

Kloo stared at me. At least, I think she stared. She still had her hat and veil on.

"That is a rather alarming question," she said.

The desk clerks would have recognized Zamboni, wouldn't they? They knew who all the mystery writers were. They had recognized and welcomed Uncle Stoppard when we arrived at the hotel early this morning.

"You're not going to sleep with that on?" Mona said.

Kloo stretched her bony frame out on a cot. "You're right. I'll get rid of the hat."

"That trek through the desert absolutely wore me out," said Babette.

Kloo turned her head toward Mona. "Would you mind not smoking in here?"

"Yes, I would mind," Mona said.

When the clatter of Mona's heels out on the hallway floor dwindled into the darkness, Kloo chuckled. "A brilliant writer, no doubt about that. But so nasty. Like a scorpion. Oh, I am sorry, Mr. Sterling. You and she are old friends, right?"

"Uh, no, we're not," Uncle Stoppard said. "We went to school together, that's all."

"Oxford?" Kloo asked.

"No, Des Moines."

Babette sat up on her cot. "I have it! It's porphyria, isn't it?"

Nada Kloo swung around. "Señora Lizardo, do you read minds?"

"No. I read magazines."

Babette explained how she had read an interview with Nada Kloo in *Murder Monthly* a few years ago. In the interview, Kloo mentioned that she suffered from porphyria, a rare blood condition that made her allergic to sunlight. That was the reason for the veil.

"Porphyria gave rise to the legend of the vampire," Babette said.

"People who have the affliction generally come out only at night," Kloo said. "Many, many years ago, before modern medicine, porphyria sufferers were forced to drink the blood of animals to stay healthy."

Great. Uncle Stoppard and I are lost in the Sahara Desert, trapped in an abandoned prison that's filled with dead French ghosts, a crazy emperor, a Russian vampire, and Mona, the bloodsucking ghoul.

I edged closer to the fire.

"Don't worry," Nada said to me. "It's not a full moon." Her chuckle sent a freezing shiver down my backbone.

Uncle Stoppard put his hand on my collar and herded me out of the room. "We'll help you look for your pilot in the morning. Uh, there's more wood over there if you need it. Good night."

"Buenas noches," Babette said.

Out in the hallway, I glanced at the bald emperor again. From this angle he seemed to be pointing at me with his right hand, the firelight painting his index finger a bloody red. To my surprise, Omar Bah was also in the hall and not praying. I guess he wasn't that worried about his soul. Bah stood next to the wall examining an ancient, flaking picture. An ancient Roman hero, wrapped in a lionskin, was fighting a fire-breathing bull. I had never seen flames painted like that. Of course they looked fake, but there was something exciting about them. The bull, at least twelve feet across and six feet high, was a swirl of scarlet and black and gold. The guy in the lionskin had grabbed onto the bull's deadly horns. Why did he wear a lionskin? As a disguise?

Bah and I must have been the first two people to look at this picture in a hundred years. It was like looking at buried treasure. The bull and the lionskin guy were an exhibit in our own private museum deep in the Teeth of Darkness. This painting was so much better than the weird stuff Uncle Stoppard dragged me to see back in Paris. And lots older. The artist must have lived long before the first Mallomar was born. Where did he find paint in this dry, empty desert? Did he bring paint and brushes all the way from ancient Rome? And did the artist ever return to Rome or did he eventually die here in Occo, far away from his friends and family?

I heard Omar Bah mumbling to himself. Something about the soul and how ancient traditions should be honored. Traditions? Like the pointy slippers and the knots and the heads of executed criminals stuck up on that wall back in Fuz? The ancient idols of Mecca used to be traditions until Muhammad the Prophet came along and smashed them all. Then he started new traditions. Were the Japanese businessmen, the newest wave of invaders to Occo, simply the next wave of traditions? Things don't always have to stay the same. For instance, Hamlet's girlfriend could be a detective. An American could win the Ruby Raven. People who were legally dead could come back to life.

Back in our room, Ota and Muhammad were sound

asleep. Abou must still be praying. I pushed my cot closer to Uncle Stoppard's and climbed in.

"Are you all right, Finn?" Uncle Stoppard asked.

"Yeah."

"You're not worried about us getting to Aznac, are you?"

"Nah," I lied. I was more worried about us ever getting to Iceland.

"Everything will turn out fine," Uncle Stoppard said.

"Promise?" I said.

"Promise."

"Okay." My eyelids felt heavy. The fire was warm and cozy.

In the middle of the night I woke up.

Shadows blacker than night filled the empty, ancient room. Embers glowed in our campfire like tiny red stars. I could barely see the other four cots. A dark shape on the floor must have been Ota Sato.

A voice—a voice I did not know—whispered in the dark. It was speaking in English (or American, as Uncle Stoppard calls it) but with a different accent. Male or female? I was sure the voice didn't belong to any of the sleeping bodies around the fire. Who was speaking? And what did it mean?

"A blur . . . no . . . no blur."

Well, was it a blur or not?

And then later, "Toss over the . . . toss over the slinky sand a rose . . . a rose."

Slinky sand? Quicksand? Who was dreaming about slinky sand and flowers?

"A rose of outer ages . . ."

Maybe the phantom of a Legionnaire officer was homesick for his garden back in France. The rose of outer ages? A ghostly flower? The room was big and hollow, full of echoes from the snoring sleepers and the rustling embers, and the voice was hardly more than a whisper. I couldn't tell which direction the words came from. But I knew they were words from an ancient place, a dead place, farther than Mortville, farther than the Farthest Mosque.

The voice died away. Silence. I listened for footsteps, for a creaking cot. Nothing. I slipped back into a dark dream in the City of Death.

8
The Razor Falls

The Sahara Desert is a good place for losing things. The next day we lost two things, and one of them was somebody's head.

The morning started with a bang—I mean, a scream.

AAAAEEEEEEEEEEEEHHHHH!!

I jumped up from my cot. Dim morning light filtered into the room from the outer halls. I was alone. The other cots were empty. Ota's straw bed was neatly covered with extra clothes brought from the bus. Abou's single yellow-and-brown shoe rested on the red floor beneath his cot. I ran into the hallway and collided with Babette running out of the women's quarters, her red hair ruffled like a flamingo nest.

"That way!" She pointed. Nada Kloo was disappearing down the corridor toward the main hall. The two of us followed her billowing white veils.

Ahead of us, on the landing that led down to the circular prison yard, stood Mona. Her harsh blue suit and brown helmet-hair were silhouetted against the pale light. She heard us behind her and swung around. Her face was drained of color. She pointed a quivering hand toward the center of the arena.

Babette gasped. "Abou!"

The guillotine was surrounded by all the men from

the bus. Except that one was missing a head. A body lay slumped against the wooden framework. A smear of blood ran from the curved neck-hole down to the headless trunk. Somehow we all stood in the center of the prison. I didn't remember running down the steps.

"Finn, you shouldn't," Babette said.

It was Muhammad. I recognized his robe. And his bare feet. The crescent moon birthmark was clearly visible. C for corpse. Muhammad's luck had run out.

Mona yelled at me. "Get away from there, kid." I took a few steps backwards, but my eyes were riveted on the dead body. In less than twenty-four hours, I had seen two. That must be some sort of record. A new smell. Blood? Was I smelling human blood for the first time? Was this the smell that attracted other creatures: cobras, lions, vultures? The body didn't look human without its head. I looked back at the guillotine blade and felt dizzy.

Ota Sato was also backing up from the guillotine, slowly, as if ungluing his feet from the ground. "Horrible," he said.

Omar Bah knelt down and carefully examined Muhammad's limbs. "This must have happened in the night." Bah glanced up at the wooden framework. "Who pulled the blade back up into position?" he said.

No one answered.

The blade had been down last night when we left the circular courtyard.

Babette frowned. "What do you suppose Muhammad was doing out here?"

"Answering the call of Mother Nature?" Mona said.

"It must have happened at lightning speed," Kloo said.

"Thirty-two feet per second per second," Abou said.

We all looked at him. This morning he was wearing some shiny lime-green pants and a clean white shirt.

Bare feet. "That's the rate of acceleration for a falling object," he explained. I was surprised Uncle Stoppard didn't mention that. He knew all about falling objects. Like Hamlet's father in *Into My Grave*.

Where was Uncle Stoppard? At that moment, I realized he wasn't in the prison yard with the rest of us.

"Uncle Stop!" I ran up the steps and tore down the hall to the men's sleeping quarters. His cot was still empty. I ran outside the temple-prison to the front steps. Maybe Uncle Stoppard was answering the call of Mother Nature. I ran down the black canyon, around the sharp bend. At the mouth of the canyon the sandstorm continued to whistle and howl. An orange wall of churning dust still curtained the entrance way. Uncle Stoppard was nowhere to be seen. No new footprints led back out into the desert.

"Uncle Stoppard!"

For the next hour, all the other mystery writers, including Mona, helped me search the prison. We tried every single one of the metal doors that faced the central yard. There are 106 doors (I counted). Some of them were rusted shut, the others led to empty cells. We found more rooms within the Roman temple building, more officers' quarters, I guessed. But no sign of Uncle Stoppard.

There was one more place to look.

"Mr. Bah," I said. I felt the dry desert air choking me. "May I borrow your flashlight, please?"

I went out into the prison yard alone. Muhammad's lifeless body still lay facedown on the sand. Facedown, I mean, if he still had a face. I saw a small scorpion skitter across his chest. A few yards away lay the open pit. I knelt down in the sand at the edge of the hole and closed my eyes. I closed them so tightly, tears squeezed out. Does Allah hear prayers only in Arabic? I opened my eyes, gripped the flashlight, thumbed the on button and peered cautiously into the darkness below me. I gasped and quickly sat back. A body! I looked again. Not a body—rocks and dirt. The skeleton of a small animal with big ears lay on its side like a dead fish. Abou's *fanak*. I noticed small holes in the sides of the pit down near the bottom. Rat holes. Or maybe snakes. Cobras? The little fox-creature must have been an unexpected feast for them.

I sat back a few feet from the pit, breathing hard, as if I had swum up through a hundred feet of dark water. Abou was standing there. I hadn't heard him come up behind me. Bare feet on sand are pretty quiet, I guess. When he put his arm around my shoulders, for some stupid reason I started to cry.

"We'll find him, Finnegan," Abou said.

"Where would he go?"

"For help?"

"How?" I said. "He's never been in the desert before. Besides, he would have told me. He wouldn't disappear like that."

"Finn—"

"We have to go looking for him."

"We have been looking."

"We have to look again," I said. I saw Mona and Omar Bah standing quietly on the stone landing, watching me.

"Perhaps," Abou whispered, "perhaps he is on a secret mission."

"Mission?" Had Abou been reading too many mysteries? "What do you mean?"

"Think of it, Finnegan. Last night, Muhammad happened to walk into a guillotine. This morning, your Uncle happens to be missing."

"You don't think he had something to do with it?"

"Your uncle? No, but perhaps he knows something about Muhammad's murder."

"Murder?"

"Careful," he said. He glanced over at Mona and Bah. "You don't believe Muhammad wandered out here by accident, do you?"

I glanced at the trunk of our former driver. "I guess not," I said.

"I do not, either."

"But you saw how easy it was to make the blade fall down."

"Yes," said Abou. "But only a fool would try it after seeing what almost happened to me. A fool or a killer." He put a hand on his throat. "Someone raised the blade back up. That was no accident."

Muhammad's foot was turning blue. The deep blue C. Why would someone kill a bus driver? With Muhammad's death, none of the mystery writers was any richer. Had Muhammad seen something suspicious last night? Is that why he was killed?

"And Uncle Stoppard?" I said.

"Perhaps he *knows* that Muhammad's death was not an accident, and is secretly carrying on an investigation."

"Like a spy?"

"In your uncle's book, remember, Ophelia only pretends to drown," Abou said. "Then she investigates the king's murder while in disguise."

Ophelia. The fake death.

"That's only a story, Abou. Uncle Stoppard's not a detective. He only writes about detectives."

"Anyone who can create *Into My Grave* knows how to solve a puzzle. And in this case, a deadly puzzle. Your uncle is an intelligent man. He can take care of himself."

Yeah, Uncle Stoppard was pretty smart. I mean *is*

smart. Lots of fans think so, too. Including weird billion-
aire fans like Truman Ravenwood. Maybe last night
Uncle Stoppard heard the strange voice mumbling
about sand and roses. Maybe he got up to investigate
and saw what actually happened to Muhammad.

"You really think so?" I said.

Abou nodded. "He is a clever man."

If, as Abou suggested, Uncle Stoppard was on a so-
called secret mission, then at least he was nearby. And
alive. His cucumber-green eyes could be gazing at us
from behind one of the metal doors that lined the prison
yard. Keeping an eye on Muhammad's murderer. Spying on us like the "dead" Ophelia spied on her
boyfriend, Hamlet.

"Let's go find some breakfast," said Abou. "And after
we eat, we'll organize another hunt for Stoppard, er,
your uncle."

"Thanks, Abou." How could I ever have thought that
he was the mad bomber? Now, with Uncle Stoppard
gone, Abou was my only real friend.

I walked back into the men's sleeping quarters, decid-
ing to search through Uncle Stoppard's clothes and
stuff. Everyone was quiet and staring at me. Babette's
eyes were red and swollen. I hate it when people try to
be nice, it only makes things worse.

Omar Bah turned to Abou. "Let's go move Muhammad's body. We can put him in one of the empty prison
cells."

I heard Ota Sato join them out in the hall. "Still no
head?" he asked.

I wasn't sure what I was looking for in Uncle Stoppard's duffel bag. Clues, I suppose. Nothing was missing.
His clothes and shoes and extra pair of glasses were still
there. His keys. The key ring had a small flashlight attached to it. I stuffed the ring into the pocket of my

khaki shorts, thinking it might be useful later on. His chukka boots—the ones he wore from the bus—were still sitting under his cot. Where would Uncle Stoppard go without his boots? I walked out into the hallway, trying to find footprints. The sandstone floor was too smooth and free of dust to find any traces of Uncle Stoppard's feet. Or anyone else's.

On the floor next to the statue of the bald Roman emperor something caught my eye. A small, crumpled-up piece of thin white paper. I unrolled it and found a scrap no bigger than my thumb. I knew it couldn't be from ancient Roman times because there was printing on it from a machine, as if the scrap had been torn from the page of a book, and the printing press was invented long after the Roman Empire rose and fell. The scrap was so small that it showed only bits of words. And one complete word:

RENDEZVOUS

I looked up at the mad Roman emperor, his right hand pointing, his blank eyes staring down the hall, past the flaking hero with the lionskin and the fire-breathing bull. If that statue could only talk.

Rendezvous meant a meeting of some kind. And some kind of meeting took place last night. But where did this scrap come from? It hadn't simply dropped out of a book, because it was crumpled into a ball. Crumpled by a human hand.

Later that morning, after Omar Bah and Abou lugged the bus driver's headless body into one of the prison cells, Babette discovered a well. Between the iron gate near the mouth of the canyon and the front steps of the prison, she found a circular tunnel that burrowed deep into the sandstone cliff. We had walked right past it last night in the dark. The tunnel led to a small, low-ceilinged cave (Omar Bah had to remove his green fooz) with a pit in the center of the floor, and instead of holding fox bones, this pit held clear, delicious-looking water. The water level was about six feet below the lip of the well, so Mona and Kloo came up with an ingenious plan. They borrowed a pair of my jeans, knotted the ends of the legs, and using strips they cut from one of the Legionnaire blankets for rope, they constructed a homemade bucket.

"This goes in my next book," Mona said.

It was weird watching my jeans hauled up from the well, heavy, bulging, and dripping with water, a tiny lake inside the waistband. Kloo looked at the back of my jeans and said, "We'll call this invention the Levi-tator." The water tasted great. Ota made origami cups from notebook paper. They dripped a little, but they worked.

The water made everyone hungry. Searching through our luggage, we collected anything that was edible. Breakfast included three apples, a box of raisins, a bag of potato chip-things, a half bag of chocolate cookies, gum, a candy bar, and a roll of butterscotch breath mints.

We ate on the front steps by the rosy red pillars. I kept shooting glances at the sharp bend in the black canyon wall, hoping that Uncle Stoppard would step into view.

"Too bad Muhammad wasn't nominated for the Ruby Raven," Mona said, chewing a raisin and smoking a cigarette at the same time. "His death would have made us all"—puff—"richer."

"That's disgusting," said Babette. "How much richer?"

"A hundred forty thousand bucks."

Abou looked up from reading *The Case of the Cairo*

Gyro, the book Nabi Neez had handed us back at the Mallomar tombs. "One hundred forty-*two* thousand," he said.

"It may not be Muhammad who died," Ota Sato said.

"What's that supposed to mean?" said Kloo.

"His head is missing. How do we know who it is?"

Mona laughed. "You're sounding like Agatha Christie, Sato."

"I know it's Muhammad," I said. I told them about the crescent-shaped birthmark on his left foot.

"Are you sure?" Mona said.

Kloo nodded. "I remember seeing that mark," she said.

Omar Bah stood up and shook out his maroon robes. "But where is the head?"

That had us all stumped.

Omar Bah smiled at us from behind his thick hedge of a beard. "The head is missing because someone took it."

"One of us," Babette said.

"Of course, one of us," Mona said. "We're the only ones here. Well,"—puff—"not *all* of us are here."

Everyone looked at me. My face felt on fire. I wanted to shout that Uncle Stoppard was not wandering around somewhere with Muhammad's head. I wanted to yell out that a stranger had been whispering in the men's quarters last night. That Uncle Stoppard might have seen a murder and was working to catch the killer. That he was probably spying on us right now. But I couldn't. Not if Uncle Stoppard was hiding out and investigating, like Abou said. I didn't want to give him away.

Babette stood up. "I don't like this talk of murder. It is totally unfounded and unnecessary. Muhammad met with a terrible, unfortunate accident. That is all."

"That's all?" Mona said.

"Muhammad stumbled out into the prison yard last night," said Babette. "And accidentally crashed into that . . . that thing."

"And Stoppard?" Mona asked.

"Mr. Sterling is lost somewhere in the prison," Abou said.

"A fugitive from justice," Mona mumbled.

"We have searched everywhere," Bah said.

"Maybe not," said Abou. "We didn't notice that tunnel leading to the well until this morning. Maybe we overlooked something."

"Perhaps Mr. Sterling went for help," Kloo said.

"Not in this storm," Mona said.

I lifted my head. The storm. "Listen," I said. I got up from the steps and ran toward the mouth of the canyon. Turning the bend, I could see that the billowing curtain of orange and yellow dust was gone. A drift of sand, six feet high, sloped across the entrance. Beyond, the Occan sky burned hot blue.

The others had followed me.

"We must look for Alexy," Kloo said.

We all climbed up the slope and gazed out on the blazing Sahara. An empty ocean of sand stretched to the horizon. No bus, no plane, no people. And no Uncle Stoppard. There were no footprints leading out of the canyon, either.

"The bus must be buried," Mona said.

"Or blown over the cliff," Kloo said.

"The map will tell us where the highway is," said Abou.

"Uncle Stoppard has the map," I said. "Remember?"

"We could guess where it is," Mona said.

Omar Bah shook his head, the great mustache wobbling. "It is too hot to go searching. We should remain here and wait to be rescued."

Hyde must have sent a rescue party out searching for us. If that creepy little guy's helicopter wasn't caught in the storm, that is.

"But how will they find us in this canyon?" I said.

Bah shrugged. "If it is Allah's will, they will find us."

Nada Kloo stayed near the mouth of the canyon, calling out for her friend. I trudged back toward the prison, alongside Abou. Babette bent over and whispered into my ear. "I have a plan," she said.

Babette invited Abou and me back to the women's sleeping quarters.

"Which one do you think?" She flourished her dresses like bullfighter capes.

"You sure like pink," I said.

Babette wrinkled her nose. "Pink? I never wear pink. This one is called Sunset Puce and this one is Whispering Rose. I'm forced to wear the more exotic colors because it is so difficult finding something that complements my brilliant hair."

Abou looked at me and winked. The dresses looked pink to him, too.

"Well, which one do you think?" Babette said.

Babette must have been trying to get my mind off Uncle Stoppard's disappearance.

"Uh, you'd look good in any one," I said.

Babette smiled brightly. "They're not for me, Finnegan. They're our distress signal!"

Babette's plan was to hang a flag or some other bright object out by the entrance of the canyon to signal any passing rescue party. Since there were no other bright objects available, she volunteered her dresses.

"You also prefer the Sunset Puce, Mr. Wittgenstein? Marvelous. That's the one I was thinking of using." I liked the word puce. It reminded me of something Uncle Stoppard would say.

I went back to my cot and slipped into the djellabah that Uncle Stoppard had bought for me at the airport. If we were going out in the desert, it might be helpful. Also, wearing it reminded me of Uncle Stop. He didn't seem quite so far away.

Babette also reminded me of Uncle Stoppard during our walk back to the canyon entrance. "I don't for a moment believe what Mona says," Babette said. "She was only trying to get my goat with her talk of murder. Murder, bah! We writers have murder on the brain." Babette patted my shoulder, her bracelets jangling. "Don't you worry. Mona doesn't believe that non-sense. She's a smart woman even if she is a beast. Such a distasteful subject. *Hola,* Mr. Sato! Have you found our bus?"

Ota Sato was scanning the horizon with a pair of binoculars. Kloo must have given up shouting for Alexy and left.

"I wasn't looking for the bus," Sato said. "I was hop-ing to see a sign of our friend Mr. Sterling."

"Anything?" I said.

"Nothing yet, I'm afraid."

Endless dunes stretched out beneath the burning sun. Uncle Stoppard had read in a book on the plane from Paris that the Sahara tribes of Occo use over thirty dif-ferent words to describe different kinds of sand. I could believe it. Gold, beige, brown, rust, silver, even shades of Babette's favorite color, swirled across the vast ocean of sand and blended into each other. Some dunes glistened like lilac petals. There were colors that Uncle Stoppard would give long and unusual names. That is, if he were here. The only objects out on the desert were two or three bluish-black boulders the size of barns. To the left and right of the canyon's mouth ran the rough black walls of the Teeth of Darkness. Above and behind us, their sharp peaks stood out like ink against the bright blue sky.

We helped Babette drape her dress on the dark rocks outside the entrance. She called it a sari, a wide rectangular piece of fabric the length of a tennis net. A camel rider or airplane pilot couldn't miss it. From a distance, it probably looked like a big pink bandage.

Babette and Ota took turns using the binoculars. Abou pulled me aside.

"Finnegan," he said. "Something Miss Lizardo said back in her room is bothering me."

"What did she say?"

"Remember when the bus tipped over and all the luggage spilled out?"

"It looked like Uncle Stoppard's bedroom," I said.

"Do you remember those wigs?"

AAAAEEEEEEEEEEEHHHHH!!

All four of us looked at each other. Mona?

We raced back to the prison.

The Queen of Crime stood in the middle of the women's sleeping quarters. Her usually perfect hair was standing on end, and her breath came in short, sharp gasps. Surrounding her, like dead leaves surrounding a bare tree, lay a circle of yellow paper.

"What," Babette said, "is going on?"

There was terror in Mona's eyes. She pointed toward her open suitcase.

A black Occan cobra lay coiled, ready to strike, on a heap of notebooks and papers in Mona's suitcase. Its flat, black head swayed back and forth. A red tongue darted between its sharp yellow fangs.

"Do something," whispered Mona.

What could we do? We all stood frozen.

The djellabah I wore was woven from thick wool. Could a cobra's fangs penetrate it? I remembered how

I had moved slowly in the bathroom at the Hôtel Splendide, without causing the cobra to strike. While everyone stood still, I slowly slipped the robe over my head. Mona stared at me. "What are you doing?" she said.

I could see Abou out of the corner of my eye, nodding his head.

I carefully gathered the thick djellabah into both hands and slowly approached the open suitcase. The case lay on Mona's cot, about two feet above the sandstone floor. The cobra's head was another foot high. Its fangs were at the same height as my chest. Would I feel a quick stab in my heart, or would the cobra be as swift as a falling guillotine blade? My knees wobbled slightly.

"Careful," whispered Mona.

The cobra turned its evil head to stare at me. Those inky black eyes. This was not a good thing. How could I throw my robe over it if it was watching me? Then Mona wiggled her hands, trying to catch the snake's attention. It worked. He swiveled back to watch her. Mona moved her hands gracefully back and forth, like a dancer. The cobra's head followed her motions, gliding back and forth.

I hurled the djellabah onto the suitcase. The cobra struck out, but got smothered in the thick robe. Mona fell back. Abou jumped forward and snapped the suitcase lid shut.

"Great work," said Abou.

"You're a brave young man," said Babette.

Mona looked up at me from the floor. "Yeah. Thanks, kid. Good aim."

Ota Sato helped the Queen of Crime to her feet. Then Mona looked down at the yellow paper scattered on the floor and exploded. "So, which one of you did this?"

"You think we planted the snake?" said Babette.

"I'm talking about my notebook."

In an angry rush, Mona told us that when she had returned to her room for a cigarette, she noticed her suitcase was unlatched. This upset her because her private notebook containing the first draft of her next Bugloop novel was in the suitcase. Mona threw open the suitcase. Her notebook was torn apart. Papers scattered everywhere. And on top of a pile of loose papers, coiled the cobra. That's when she screamed.

"Why don't you use a laptop like everyone else?" said Babette.

Mona sat on the floor, reassembling the loose sheets of paper she had scattered in her anger. "Because I don't write like everyone else!"

"Is there anything we can salvage?" Abou said.

Mona looked bewildered. "I don't believe it—all my notes are here."

"So they weren't stolen, then," I said.

Mona's voice was calm and precise. "My suitcase *was* tampered with. And someone went through my things. But instead of simply taking my entire notebook, someone tore out all the sheets that I had written on, threw them back in the suitcase, and took what was left."

"Empty sheets?" Abou said.

"I number the pages as I go," Mona said. "And they're all here." She glared at Babette.

"Weird," I said.

"I don't get it," Abou said. "Surely Miss Squeer's writing would be more valuable than blank sheets of paper."

Babette grinned and winked at me. "Obviously you haven't read her lately."

"I heard that!" Mona snapped.

"Then hear this!" said the Spanish Queen. "I didn't touch your notebook. Or your suitcase."

"Someone did," Mona said. "Someone in this room."

That didn't narrow things down much, since everyone

from the bus was in the room. Everyone except Muhammad and Uncle Stoppard.

"I was in the prison yard," Omar Bah said. "Searching for, er, the head."

"I was out by the canyon entrance," said Kloo.

"We all were," I said.

"I was with Mr. Wittgenstein and Sterling's nephew," Ota Sato said. "We were helping Ms. Lizardo spread her dress while she was on the rocks."

"Everyone's got an alibi," said Mona. "But one of you is lying." She clutched the loose yellow pages of her notebook to her chest.

"What should we do about the cobra?" I asked. "Should we leave it locked in your suitcase?"

Mona's mouth formed a perfect O. The O expanded in slow motion, like a pupil in a dark room.

"You're not going to scream again, are you?" Kloo said.

Mona pointed past us. I swung around.

A stranger slouched against the doorway. A strange man with long blond hair tied in a ponytail, a leather jacket, and a gun.

9

Footnotes to Murder

The strange man and Nada Kloo ran to each other.
"Nada," he exclaimed. The blond man winced when she
embraced him.

"What is it?" she said.

"It is nothing, Nada, my darling."

Kloo pulled him into the room. "Come and sit down,
Alexy. Everyone, this is my pilot, Alexander Bletz. Oh!"
The guy stumbled and almost fell onto the cot. Underneath his open leather jacket, his left arm hung in a
homemade sling.

"It is nothing," he said. "Nothing."

"What's with the gun, Bletz?" said Abou.

"I did not know what to expect," Bletz said. "I saw a
pink banner out by the entrance and thought someone
might be here—"

"It's not pink," Babette said.

"—but then I saw the temple. I did not know who
might be here . . ."

"What pink banner?" Omar Bah said.

"Nada," said Bletz, "is there any water?"

Ota Sato ran to get more water from the well. Alexander Bletz undid his ponytail, and long golden hair fell
over his shoulders. He removed a knapsack that he had
been carrying and dropped it on the marble floor. It was
marked with strange letters:

ОПЕЛ
24Г–ZΘ447

"What language is that?" I asked.

"Russian," Alexander said, "It is the name of my plane, the *Eagle*. And those are my plane's ID numbers."

"But the L is upside down."

"It's the Cyrillic alphabet," Kloo said. "We use it in Russia like you Europeans use the Roman alphabet."

"I'm not European," I said. But no one heard me. Then it struck me. Muhammad's foot.

"Abou," I whispered. "Follow me." I hurried out of the room and stopped next to the painting of the fire-breathing bull.

"What is it, Finn? You have something mysterious on your mind."

"Yeah, and Muhammad has something mysterious on his foot."

"His foot?"

"That Russian guy's knapsack made me think of it. You know how the L looked upside down?"

"Actually, it's not an L," Abou said. "It's a *g*, like the Greek gamma."

"How do you know so much?"

"I go to college."

"Well, that gamma thing made me think of Muhammad. When I saw his body this morning, I noticed the birthmark on his left foot."

"The crescent moon?"

"Right, shaped like the letter C. That's how I knew for sure that it was Muhammad, because last night, I saw the C on his foot when I helped him off with his shoes. But, last night, Muhammad was sitting on his cot, facing me."

"Yes?"

"And today, Muhammad's body was facedown. But the C looked the same!"

"It is the same C," Abou said.

"No, it can't be. If Muhammad was lying on the floor facedown, then the C should look flipped over, too. Backwards. Reversed."

A funny light came over Abou's face. "If it's not Muhammad's foot, chances are it's not his body, either."

Goosebumps prickled my arms. "Let's go look," I said.

Abou and I quietly entered the vast prison yard. Sunlight poured in from directly overhead.

"Bah and I carried him over there," Abou said.

We walked over to a cell on the floor level of the prison, ten doors down from the stone landing. I pulled open the wooden door. The ancient hinges squealed. The cell was only as big as my bedroom back home. A single cot was pushed against a side wall. On the cot lay the remains of our bus driver beneath a dusty green blanket. I opened the door wider to let in more light. The air in the room felt stuffy and hot.

"Which end is which?" I said.

Abou pointed. "I think those are his feet."

Slowly, I lifted the blanket. Two pale, bluish feet, toes pointed toward the ceiling. Like Nabi Neez's feet sticking out from beneath the pillar. My own feet felt weak.

"You were right," Abou whispered. The crescent moon birthmark on Muhammad's left foot was now pointing to the left. It was backwards. If I had watched the body being carried away, I might have noticed the difference. But I had seen the birthmark while Muhammad's body was still lying on the sand floor.

"Let's try this," Abou said. He pulled a handkerchief from his green pants pocket and wiped it against the dead foot. The birthmark smeared. Abou stared at me, then he rubbed harder and the mark began to grow fainter. "Ink," he said. We both took a deep breath.

"Someone wanted us to think this is Muhammad," I said.

Imagine someone in the dead of night, drawing a birthmark on a corpse's foot. A foot that would have been warm to the killer's touch.

"I thought it odd when you first told us about Muhammad asking for help removing his shoes," Abou said.

"Why odd?"

"Well, in Islamic countries, it's not done. Showing someone the sole of your foot is considered highly rude. In your country it would be like, um, dropping your trousers."

"You mean, mooning someone?"

"Er, yes."

I looked at Mohammad's half-erased crescent moon.

"Who is this?" I asked.

"Well, it's a man," Abou said, lifting and lowering the blanket quickly. "But with the head missing, we may never be sure who."

A buzzing sound filled the air when Abou had lifted the blanket, and then faded when the blanket was lowered. Flies? It sounded like a million of them. The blanket twitched slightly where the head should have been. Creeping, crawling flies. I leaned against the wall and gagged.

"Finn, you okay?"

"Great."

"Earlier today, I was going to tell you something that I had observed. Before we heard Mona's scream."

"Can we get out of this room, Abou?"

We closed the cell door behind us. We were alone in the prison yard.

"Those wigs that were scattered among the clothes and luggage," Abou said. "Whose are they?"

I slid down against the prison wall and sat in the sand. "They belong to Babette."

"Do they?" Abou said. "This morning Babette said it was so hard for her to find colors that matched her brilliant red hair, remember? If she wore wigs, she wouldn't have to worry about that. She could change her hair to match her outfit. But that's not what she does. Babette likes her hair color, so she finds clothes that will match."

"Mona?"

"Not Mona," Abou said. "She's not the type to wear a wig. And Nada Kloo was not traveling with us. None of her luggage was on the bus."

"Men don't wear wigs."

"Usually, no. Unless it's a disguise."

Disguise. Like Ophelia from *Into My Grave*. That reminded me of Uncle Stoppard. I glanced back at the body on the cot. The feet were big like Uncle Stoppard's. Though I didn't want to, I forced myself to stand and walk over to the body again. I lifted the side of the blanket. Blue arms and fingers. Uncle Stoppard has freckles all over his arms. This body did not. I breathed a sigh of relief and almost started crying again..

"It's not him, is it?" Abou asked.

I shook my head.

"I was afraid to ask," Abou said. "But I'm glad we know." He handed me his hankie.

The body was not Muhammad or Uncle Stoppard. Whose corpse was lying under the Legionnaire blanket? And why make us believe it was Muhammad? I sat back down outside the cell and blew my nose.

"It fits the pattern," Abou said.

"What pattern?"

"Mystery writers. First, your uncle is threatened with a poisoned dart and is almost blown up with an explosive package sent through the mail. The palm tree at the hotel narrowly misses wiping out several writers at once. Nabi Neez is crushed by a falling pillar. Brentano Zamboni disappears."

"Do you think Zamboni was the body they found stuffed in the urn?"

Abou shook his head. "Not sure. But Muhammad doesn't fit. Why kill a bus driver?"

"But you said it did fit the pattern."

"Because it is *not* Muhammad," Abou said. "To fit the pattern, another writer would have been killed."

Although the noon sun was blazing down into the prison, I got goosebumps again.

"This body is one of the writers?" I said. "But everyone's still here. Except for Uncle Stoppard, I mean. And that isn't his body."

"Have you started reading that book Nabi gave us back at Mallomar?"

"The Case of the Cairo Gyro?"

"Yes, the story revolves around a stolen gyroscope and the Scientific Detective is called in to investigate. That's the only name he's ever given—the Scientific Detective, S.D.—because he's so logical and organized and scientific about his detecting. At the beginning of each case, he writes down all the questions that bug him, everything he doesn't understand. And those questions help him decide where to look next in his investigation."

It was a good idea. We walked back up the stone landing and sat in the shade of the doorway. In a few minutes, our list in Abou's pad looked like this:

WHAT BUGS US:
1. Where is Uncle Stoppard?
2. Who was killed last night? (or, same question: Who was Muhammad?)
3. Who was killed at the hotel? (Zamboni?)
4. Who was the person Finn heard running in the Mallomar Tombs?
5. Who brought the wigs and why?
6. Why wasn't a title listed next to Omar Bah's name on the telegram?
7. If he's not dead, what happened to Brentano Zamboni?
8. Who stole the blank pages from Mona's note-book and why?

Abou looked at the list. "Eight questions. One for each of us here in the prison."

How would the Scientific Detective have handled this? Or Ophelia?

"I have another thought," Abou said. "But I don't like it. The body we examined is a fake. I mean, it's a fake Muhammad."

"That's why the head is missing," I said.

"Right, so we wouldn't know that it wasn't Muham-mad. Okay, so where is the *real* Muhammad? Someone's dead, someone that we're supposed to *think* is Muham-mad. But where is our bus driver?"

"Hiding out, like Uncle Stoppard?"

"Why? And there's still the problem with the wigs," Abou said.

I looked at our list. "There are still a lot of problems."

The wigs we saw in the bus yesterday could have be-longed to anyone. Anyone who was planning to use them as a disguise. A man or a woman.

"Disguises are tricky," I said. "I mean, they're difficult."

"What do we know for sure?" Abou said. "We know that Muhammad is missing and someone is dead."

We also knew the list of nominees for the Ruby Raven was growing shorter, name by name. Nabi Neez, Brent Zamboni, Uncle Stoppard . . . dead or missing or hiding. I gazed out at the rust-colored walls of the arena-sized prison yard. Did a pair of eyes look back at us from behind a closed metal door? Friendly eyes or frightened eyes?

"Maybe we're not alone in the prison, after all," I said. "Maybe the body belongs to someone who arrived here before us. Or after us. Maybe the body is someone we don't know."

I thought of adding a ninth question to our list: Who is Alexander Bletz?

10
Dark Passage

He's the life of the party, that's who he is.

When Abou and I returned to our quarters, we walked in on a feast. Alexander Bletz had brought food with him from his plane. Weird food. His knapsack overflowed with tins of caviar and salmon, spicy cheese, fancy crackers, fruit preserves, and two bottles of French champagne.

"We actually brought three bottles," said Kloo. During lunch, she kept her veil on. She lifted it only slightly whenever she took a drink, and then I caught glimpses of a pale, feminine face. "We'll break out the third when I win the Ruby Raven."

"Fat chance," Mona mumbled, crunching on a cracker.

Bletz told us about his adventures in the sandstorm, after he and Kloo were separated. He had stumbled into a pink rock wall and figured it surrounded the village they had seen from the air. He felt his way along the wall and came to a gateway. He didn't expect the gateway to have steps leading down on the inside; that's when he stumbled and landed on his arm. It wasn't a village, Bletz said. He only found a small white building no larger than a shed, a few palm trees, and a sandy courtyard surrounded by the pink wall.

"It's a *kouba*," said Abou. "A burial ground for a Muslim saint. Isn't that right, Mr. Bah?"

Omar Bah quietly sipped his champagne.

"Looks like I traded one tomb for another," Bletz joked.

"A burial ground," Kloo said. "And I was hoping for a shower and a real bed."

"We'll be in Aznac, soon," said Bletz.

"How can you be so certain?" Mona asked.

"I'm sure they sent out search parties. The Fuz airport radioed ahead to the landing strip in Aznac to let them know my plane was coming. It's standard procedure, with only one route through the mountains— the same route the highway follows. We'll be rescued very soon."

"It's been almost twenty-four hours," Mona said.

"Your plane doesn't work?" I said.

Bletz shook his long golden hair. "The left wing is damaged."

"Could we use the radio?" asked Babette.

"Broken," Bletz said.

Bletz's compass wasn't broken, though. He said the *Eagle* was south-southwest of Mortville prison. Once the sandstorm stopped, he said, he easily spied the pink banner against the black cliffs through his binoculars.

"It's not that far off the highway," Bletz said.

"It's not pink," Babette said.

"What about Uncle Stoppard?" I asked.

"Stoppard Sterling of *Into My Grave?*" said Bletz. "He's your uncle? Cool! I love that part in his book where the dead girlfriend comes back disguised as a guy and solves the mystery. Oh, I hope I didn't spoil the ending for anyone."

"We're familiar with the plot," Mona said.

Nada Kloo explained to Bletz that Uncle Stoppard had mysteriously disappeared. With help and interruptions from everyone else, she also told Bletz about

Muhammad, I mean, the body we found this morning at the guillotine. Abou and I shared a glance. We had decided not to tell anyone about the fake birthmark. At least, not yet. We were worried that someone eating lunch with us knew far more about the death of "Muhammad" than they were willing to tell.

Alexander Bletz reminded me of Uncle Stoppard's cop buddy back in Minneapolis, Jared Lemon-Olsen. He was tall and athletic, and he didn't seem to let his bruised or busted arm keep him from having fun. After polishing off three apples, a peach, a pair of pears, a handful of dates, a tin of red caviar, and half a bottle of champagne, Bletz jumped to his feet, swept his long golden hair behind his ears with his good hand and said, "Who's in for the search?"

"What search?" Kloo said. "You're here now."

"For Mr. Sterling," he said, smiling at me.

"Soon as I make a pit stop," I said.

Never eat caviar in the desert. Or salmon. They only make you thirsty, which is not a good thing if there's not much water nearby. I ran down the front steps of the prison and made my way to the tunnel Babette had discovered earlier that day.

I remembered Uncle Stoppard's key ring in my pocket. The miniature flashlight was bright enough to light my way to the well. I picked up my bucket-jeans from where they were lying on the other side of the well and lowered them into the pit for a drink. They must have been four times heavier when filled up with water.

As I raised the Levi-tator to the edge of the pit and was raising it to my lips by holding on to the wet belt-loops, I saw a head in the water. I gasped. Muhammad's head? No, Omar Bah's head, his great mustache wings spread.

"Sorry if I startled you."

Omar Bah was standing on the other side of the water well. I had seen the reflection of his head in the small pool of the homemade bucket.

"You didn't startle me," I said. My heart was still pounding.

I flashed a beam of light at him. Behind him was a dark hole, the mouth of another tunnel. He must have seen something in my expression, because he swung around.

"Abou was right," he said. "There may be many hiding places we have overlooked while searching for your uncle." Omar Bah turned his glittery gold spectacles toward me and gestured with his hand. "Shall we?"

"Did you want some water?" I said.

He shook his head. "I was accompanying Mr. Bletz when we passed by this tunnel and I saw a light at the end of it. Your flashlight. Lead on, young man."

The tunnel led deep into the Teeth of Darkness. It was smooth and rounded like Babette's tunnel, but the black sandstone soon gave way to the brownish red sandstone that the temple was carved from. The color of dried blood. Bah was directly behind me. I could feel the brush of his long robes against my ankles as we trudged through that passageway into the unknown. Two heavy hands grabbed my shoulders. I shouted.

"Sorry again," said Omar Bah. "I tripped over my robe on this slope. The tunnel seems to be heading upwards."

"And it's getting skinnier," I said. If the tunnel grew any skinnier, Omar Bah would have trouble following me. That wouldn't be so bad. Unfortunately, the tunnel began to widen. The sides grew straighter, flatter like walls.

Up ahead, I heard a flapping sound. Bats? The flashlight beam fell on an old flag on a wooden pole set into the sandstone wall. It must have been a Legionnaire flag because of the red and green stripes.

I sighed. "I thought it was a bat."

"Do not worry," said Omar Bah. "I'm sure you will find no, as you say, yucky bats in here to bother you, Master Zwake."

What did Nabi call them? Rhino something bats? Those black, hanging rodents from the Mallomar Tombs. Yuck was right. I remembered how my words echoed under the gateway to the tombs like an invisible, bouncing ball.

Why was the flag flapping? A slight breeze stirred though the tunnel, a breeze that we hadn't felt earlier. There must be an opening nearby.

A constellation of stars glowed dimly up ahead of us. But instead of shining above us, the stars were straight out in front of us. How could it be night already? As we walked closer, we found the stars were actually holes, the thickness of pencils, drilled through a sandstone wall. Pinholes. Seven holes pierced the wall, the bright light shining behind the wall made them appear like a constellation. One of the holes was low enough on the wall for me to spy through.

An ancient Roman hero, wrapped in a lionskin, was fighting a fire-breathing bull. Wow, a second bull painting! I could tell from the hero's painted muscles and the bull's nostril flames that it was made by the same painter as the first one. Wait, what if this was the first one? Where were we? The tunnel had led us back along the canyon and into the temple. Bah was inches from me, peering through another pencil hole. I glanced up at him. There was enough light from the seven holes to see his face; it was not a happy face. He was staring intently, angrily, through the peephole.

The Legionnaire flag flapped quietly behind us.

Cold fingers touched the back of my neck. Not real ones, this time. It was the thought of the flag.

Bats.

Omar Bah had not been at the Mallomar Tombs the morning Nabi Neez was killed. He had stayed back at the hotel. So how did Bah know that I had called the bats "yucky"? The only people standing under the archway at that time were me, Uncle Stoppard, Abou, Nabi, and Babette. And the man in the orange *djellabah,* the stranger whose features were hidden by his hood. Omar Bah could not have known I used that particular American word to describe bats, unless he had been there himself.

"This appears to be a dead end," said Omar Bah.

"What?"

"We'll need to retrace our steps. We can't go any farther."

How did Bah get back to the Hôtel Splendide from the Mallomar Tombs? He must have supplied his own transportation, as Mona suspected Brent Zamboni had done.

"You need to go first," Omar Bah said. "You have the light."

Back through that long, dark tunnel again?

"Do you think anyone can hear us on the other side of this wall?" I said.

"Everyone is out searching for your uncle," said Bah.

Maybe Mona had stayed back in her room, working on her notebook. She might be able to hear us.

"Hello!" I shouted into one of the pencil holes.

Omar Bah looked at me strangely. "We need to go back," he said. He took a step and walked into the Legionnaire flag. "What is—? Oh." He chuckled. "I can see how this would remind you of a bat." Omar Bah stopped chuckling. He stared at me. He must have been thinking of the Mallomar Tombs, too.

"Hello!" I shouted again.

"It's no use," said Omar Bah. "We have to turn around."

Why didn't Omar Bah tell us he had been up at the Mallomars that day? Why keep it a secret? Unless he was the person who pushed the pillar. Those hands of his were huge. Strong enough to knock someone out. Strong enough to lift an unconscious body up against a guillotine and hold it there while the heavy blade came crashing down. Wouldn't there be blood everywhere? Of course, Bah wasn't wearing his suit from yesterday. His vanilla suit probably looked more like raspberry.

"Why are you waiting?" asked Omar Bah. He reached out and detached the ancient flagpole from the wall. "It's heavier than I would have guessed," he said.

I backed up against the wall.

Omar Bah stepped toward me. "See?" he said. "A flag. No bats."

The cool sandstone felt firm against my back.

Omar Bah wouldn't kill me, would he? It would be too easy to suspect him. Bletz must have seen him walk into the tunnel leading to the well. Unless Bah was lying, and no one else knew where he was.

For that matter, why kill Muhammad here in the prison? Whoever is the murderer must know that the list of suspects is a short list. There were only eight of us in the prison the night Muhammad was killed. Nine now, with Bletz. Why not wait until we got to Aznac? In Aznac, a killer could blend in with the crowds.

"Why are you afraid?" said Bah.

"I—I'm not," I said.

"Then why are you backing away? Look out!"

Light flooded the tunnel. I was falling through space. Another head was staring at me. A head with a dark helmet of hair, a sharp nose, and thin lips. Mona Trafalgar-Squeer.

"You all right, kid?" she asked.

The sandstone wall had rotated silently outward. I, or Omar Bah, must have touched a switch or something. It was like those hidden passages in old scary movies, or Babette's murder novels. I had fallen against the wall as it rotated and fell on the floor of the hallway. The bald emperor stood quietly watching. Mona was puffing purple cigarette smoke into my face.

She and Bah helped me to my feet.

"What's that?" said Mona.

"We think it is a Legionnaire flag," said Omar Bah. "We found it inside the tunnel. I was going to give it to the young man here."

"Give it to me?" I said.

"I thought Americans love souvenirs," he said.

I backed up against the painting of the bull and the lionskinned hero. "You—you said the bats were yucky."

"Pardon?"

"Yucky, yucky. You said the bats were yucky."

Both Mona and Bah looked confused. "I don't remember," said Omar Bah.

Finn, keep your mouth shut. A voice whispered through my brain. A loud voice, Uncle Stoppard's voice.

"You don't look well," said Mona. "Why don't you have something more to eat?" She pulled me into the women's quarters and sat me down on one of the cots. "Caviar?" she said.

"Uh, no, thanks."

"Sorry. I guess kids don't like caviar." She handed me an apple. "Eat that before you get up. And don't make any noise, I'm trying to organize these notes." Mona sat, puffing, on her own cot, shuffling her yellow note sheets into four separate piles.

Time passed slowly. It took me a week to finish eating the apple. That's how it felt, anyway. I felt a lump on the back of my head where I had hit the floor. Would I get a concussion? Now I sounded like Uncle Stoppard. He was the healthiest person I knew, but he was always worried about getting hurt.

Could Uncle Stoppard have found a secret passage last night? Maybe he had simply gotten up to answer the call of Mother Nature, leaned against a hidden switch somewhere, and then found himself locked inside a secret room.

When Abou got back from the search, it was growing darker. We'd have to spend another night in the prison. I joined him in the men's quarters and helped him build a fire. Bah was nowhere around.

"I have more questions to add to our list," I said.

9. Who is Alexander?
10. Who was the guy in the orange hood at Mallomar?
11. How did Omar Bah know the word "yucky"?

"Yucky?" said Abou. "Is that English?"

"Yeah, it means horrible, gross, disgusting."

"Like American peanut butter," said Abou.

"Uh, okay." I told Abou what had happened to me in the tunnel with Omar Bah.

"So you think Bah is not Bah? Hmm, I could ask him something in Arabic," said Abou. "Or French. And if he didn't understand me, we'd know he was a fake."

"We could look at the bottom of his foot and see if there's a birthmark."

"Oh, no," said Abou. "You do not look at the bottom of a Muslim's foot, remember?"

That was why the clerk back at the airport store didn't want me to try those funny-looking slippers on. He thought it was rude.

"It is our feet which lead us to God or the Devil," Abou said.

How would Omar Bah know about my feeling for the bats? He must have been the Man in the Orange Hood. Could it have been Muhammad? We still didn't know his full story. Or, maybe someone else was in disguise at the Mallomar Tombs. Bah was easy to impersonate, with his long flowing robes and his thick, black beard. It would be equally easy, though, to impersonate Babette Lizardo. Babette has a distinctive appearance—brilliant red hair, floppy hats, gobs of jewelry, those colorful non-pink gowns she wore. She certainly carried enough luggage and makeup to change her looks. Could she be, as Uncle Stoppard would say, the genuine article?

The only other people at Mallomar that day were Abou and Uncle Stoppard and me. Had another figure lurked in the shadows?

"Do you think the killer will strike again tonight?" I asked.

"We needn't worry about it," said Abou. "You and I are not mystery writers."

Yeah, we weren't writers. But then, neither was Muhammad. Right?

"I'm sure everyone will take precautions tonight and be extra vigilant."

Everyone congregated in the men's quarters that night for dinner, at which we finished up the last of Alexander Bletz's supplies. Omar Bah didn't seem nervous at all. He almost never looked in my direction. And when we both described our adventure with the tunnel and the rotating wall, he sounded perfectly natural. Was I imagining things? Maybe I used the word *yucky* some other time, and Bah remembered it because it was so strange. Writers are like word magnets. I learned that from Uncle Stoppard.

No signs of Uncle Stoppard were found.

"I'll search again in the morning," said Bletz. He seemed the type of guy who never gives up. When we got ready for bed, I told him he could use my cot. I'd sleep in Uncle Stoppard's.

Abou and I were the only ones heading for bed. Everyone else had walked over to the women's quarters and stood chatting and laughing.

"I'm sure that tomorrow the rescue party will arrive," said Abou, carefully folding up his pants beneath his cot. "They will help us find your uncle."

"Yeah, I hope so."

I gazed up at the dried-blood sandstone ceiling and listened to the crackle of the flames. I listened to the laughter next door and thought of Uncle Stoppard without food or water, without a fire to keep him warm. Was it possible to freeze to death in the middle of the Sahara Desert? I shivered beneath my blanket.

11

Bodies Lost and Found

Voices woke me.

Not the mysterious whisperer of roses and quicksand, but the mystery writers next door. A loud explosion of their late-night laughter burst in on my dreams. It was late, our fire had burned down to a smolder. I rolled over on my cot and saw that Abou was missing. His blanket lay at the foot of his cot. His folded-up pants were gone.

I got up—the stone floor chilled my bare feet—and tiptoed over toward the other room.

Standing in the dark hallway, under the watchful gaze of the mad emperor, I heard Mona's voice. "Your turn, Bah." Cautiously, I peered around the corner of the doorway.

The mystery writers were sitting in a circle on the cots around a small, dying fire. It reminded me of a campfire up in the Minnesota north woods. Alexander Bletz, the life of the party, kept passing a large bottle of champagne around the circle.

"*Sí, sí,* Senor Bah," said Babette, clapping her hands and jangling her bracelets. "Let's hear an Occan ghost story."

Omar Bah's little spectacles twinkled redly in the smoldering firelight. His thick beard was the color of ink. He sat silently, ignoring the others.

"Come on, Omar," said Alexander Bletz. "A spooky story. Everyone else did one."

The huge bull-like Occan rose from the cot where he was sitting. "Forgive me, Señorita Lizardo. But since I tell stories to frighten and amuse for a living, I have grown out of the habit of telling them for free." He sat down.

"Listen, Bah. We *all* tell stories for a living," said Mona. "That's why we're here."

"It's just fun," added Alexander Bletz.

"Speaking of stories," said Nada Kloo, her bony hands adjusting her gauzy veil, "When I received my invitation to this event, I noticed there was no title printed next to your name, Monsieur Bah. A typo, I presume?"

A murmur went round the circle of writers. I remembered Uncle Stoppard pointing out that same typo back in my bedroom in Minneapolis.

"Which of your books earned you the nomination for the Ruby Raven, Mr. Bah?" asked Ota Sato. "I was under the impression that you hadn't published anything new in the last few years."

"You are right, Sato. Bah has not published anything recently."

Weird. Why did some people refer to themselves by name? Finn would never do that.

"Why the nomination, Bah?" asked Bletz. "Did you slip a few Occan drachmas to the award committee?" In the dim light, I could see a grin on Bletz's face.

"I am not privy to the inner workings of the Nevermore Society," said Bah.

"There is no society," said Mona. "It's only Truman Ravenwood."

"Then he must be crazy," said Nada Kloo.

"He's crazy all right," said Mona. Then she started telling a story about how Truman Ravenwood liked playing practical jokes. While Mona chatted, I watched the faces of the other writers as they listened to her.

All of the nominees for the Ruby Raven were experts in murder. They wrote about it, thought about it, researched sneaky and efficient methods of killing people. Like a guillotine in an abandoned prison! These writers were two-legged encyclopedias of death. Uncle Stoppard once told me that a good mystery writer dreams about death. One of the writers listening to Mona, or maybe Mona herself, did more than simply dream about it last night. One of them hauled up that heavy French blade sitting in the courtyard of the prison, and then dropped its cold, deadly weight on Muhammad. Or whoever he was.

Babette was giggling at Mona's story. *"Sí, sí,"* she said. "Truman is such a dear, amusing man." Babette seems so friendly, sometimes even silly. Is that a disguise? Acting a certain way can be as effective a disguise as wearing a mask and whiskers. Perhaps Babette pretended to be scared or worried last night, and woke up Muhammad, asking him to help her. She tricked him into going out into the dark courtyard and then pushed him in the way of the guillotine's blade. The Spanish Queen of Crime didn't look strong, but she was plump. Her weight could have thrown Muhammad off balance. Were any of those gold question marks around Babette's pink neck splattered with bus-driver blood?

Ota Sato wasn't big, but he was a former sumo wrestler. An expert in attacking and pushing and pulling. He'd have no problem shoving someone onto the deadly guillotine. From my vantage point at the doorway in the hall, I watched him listening intently to Mona, sipping from a little origami paper cup of champagne. His small, slender frame was as still as a cat. But cats can spring and jump in the blink of an eye. Uncle Stoppard doesn't like cats.

"Truman Ravenwood might be crazy," said Abou, "but he knows mysteries. He used to be a writer, then a publisher. People in the industry respect his opinion."

"Well, he certainly lost my respect," said Mona, "when he nominated old Bah Bah Black Sheep here."

Abou sat on a cot, swinging his legs. Could he be the killer? Impossible. I could tell by looking at Abou's honest face, by watching his warm brown eyes. He could never be mean enough to kill someone.

Who could tell what was in Nada Kloo's eyes? That stupid veil was always in the way. While Mona was talking, Nada slipped over to another part of the room and rummaged through Alexander Bletz's knapsack for a tin of caviar. She passed between the fire and me, and for an instant I caught a profile of her face, the shadows of a sharp nose and a strong, bony chin. She took another step, and her face became invisible once more. Did Nada Kloo truly have a disease that made her allergic to sunlight? Or was she trying to hide her face because it was too familiar? Would we recognize her as someone else? As a famous killer? Mystery writers spend enormous amounts of time researching murder and crime. I'll bet the faces of all the known murderers in the world have been memorized by this bunch.

Maybe Kloo's mummy-like robes disguised a strong, muscular body. A body that would have no trouble raising a heavy metal blade, or burying someone in a big pot.

No one knew much about Kloo's companion, Alexander Bletz. All we knew about the blond pilot was that he had a gun. And he was fun to be around. Bletz seemed like a good guy to me. It was his idea to go hunting for Uncle Stoppard again. He laughed and joked. He was the only person here in Mortville who could get away with poking fun at Mona and not have her throw something at him. Bletz was sort of in love with Nada, I guess. Would he kill for her? Why would a big strong guy like Bletz love a scrawny, bony thing like Nada Kloo? Was he hoping to share in the wealth of the Ruby Raven? A million bucks would buy a lot of champagne. And a new plane.

"Ravenwood is notorious for avoiding photographers," Mona was saying.

"He's also notorious for the famous Ruby Raven banquets," said Babette. "One year it was baked polar bear."

Polar bear?

Mona was sitting with her back mostly to me. Her helmet of dark brown hair and her strong shoulders were silhouetted by the warm red fire. No one in the world could spin a puzzle like Mona Trafalgar-Squeer. Uncle Stoppard came close. Mona could dream up all sorts of ways to kill people. But Mona was rude. Uncle Stoppard once told me that murderers tended not to be rude or loud or obnoxious. It was usually the quiet people who killed. Rude, loud people got all the bad feelings, all the poison, out of their systems by being mean all the time. Quiet people let the poison grow stronger and stronger.

Mona was also ambitious. She wanted to win that bird. Last year's winner was Brent Zamboni, but Zamboni was missing this time around. Had Mona gotten rid of him back in the hotel? What about that cobra in the bathroom at the Hôtel Splendide? That was a scene right out of one of Mona's books. In fact, there was a snake in one of her books, *Death Ties the Knot*. Maybe the snake belonged to Mona. Maybe she brought it in her suitcase, and merely pretended to be surprised by it. Mona had so much practice killing people in books, she would be an expert in real life. And an expert in throwing people off her track.

Then there was Omar Bah. He creeped me out. Huge as a mountain, powerful as an ox, he could lift me or Ota Sato or Nada Kloo with one massive hand, if he had wanted to. And who knows what he wanted? Why was his name missing a book title on the Ruby Raven telegrams? Bah was quiet and mysterious. Too quiet. Was the poison growing silently within him?

I kept staring at the faces in that dim chamber. One of those faces belonged to a killer. A killer who was responsible for Uncle Stoppard's disappearance. I turned away from the room, leaned against the cold stone wall, and closed my eyes.

My stomach growled. Was Uncle Stoppard hungry, too?

Mona's voice grew loud. "I don't get it. Why would a respected figure like Truman Ravenwood nominate a has-been like Bah? And why does the ceremony have to take place in an oversized litter box called Occo?"

"Litter box!" boomed Bah.

All at once, the room exploded. It was like the scene on the bus right before we tipped over. Bah started bellowing, people began shouting things. Stomping, angry footsteps approached the door. I scurried across the hallway and jumped into my cot. I pulled the blanket up to my chin and closed my eyes. Squeaks, rumbles, and grumbles accompanied the men as they quickly settled for sleep. Too bad Uncle Stoppard had to miss the party. I think he would have liked it.

The next morning I got up early. I decided to search the circular courtyard again, alone this time. Some of the doors we tried yesterday had been stuck shut. I was going to borrow Omar Bah's flashlight and see what I could observe through the closed doors' barred windows. But, Bah was not in his cot. Ota Sato's blankets on the floor were also empty.

I helped myself to Bah's flashlight under his cot and walked out to the prison yard. Crunching sounds echoed throughout the vast arena. Quick steps. Ota Sato was in a green jogging suit, running around the curving track of the courtyard. He was jogging alongside the far wall, on the opposite side of the guillotine from where I stood. He waved at me. I waved back and noticed the guillotine's blade had remained down. No one had raised it again after discovering Muhammad's headless trunk. Was that more blood on the sand by the guillotine? I walked closer. The blood wasn't the same deep red as the smear on the blade, or the dried pool where Muhammad's body had fallen. Uncle Stoppard would have called the color maroon.

It wasn't blood, but a flowing robe. Omar Bah's robes, lying along the ground, had snagged on the lip of the pit.

Stepping over to the black hole, I shined Bah's own flashlight into the depths. I must have jumped or yelled. Ota Sato came running over. "What's wrong?" he said.

Then he saw it, too. The Occan mystery writer lay in a broken heap at the bottom of the pit. Beard, glasses, fooz, and all lay silent among the fox bones. I know it sounds terrible, but I felt relieved, glad that it wasn't Uncle Stoppard's body. Sato immediately ran back into the prison, yelling for help. I looked down at Bah a second time. His arms were bent at weird, unnatural angles. It was a good thing I hadn't eaten anything for breakfast yet. My stomach got all queasy and I almost hurled into the pit.

Ota Sato returned with the others. Nada Kloo could barely speak, she was so upset. She kept shaking her head and whispering hoarsely, "I cannot believe it."

"Tragic," said Babette. "Such a tragic accident."

"Accident?" Mona said. "This is the most accident prone group of people I've ever seen in my life. Remind me to never get on an elevator with you, Babs."

A loud buzzing sound came from overhead.

"Look!" cried Ota Sato, pointing upward. A small plane gleamed in the pale blue sky. "Quickly! The entrance."

We all rushed out of the prison yard, up the steps, through the hall, down the other steps, into the canyon, finally reaching the entrance panting and sweating to beat the band.

"I don't see it," said Abou.

"There," said Mona. "On the other side of that boulder."

The buzzing grew louder. The small plane flew into view from behind one of the barn-sized rocks and soared over our heads. We jumped up and down and yelled and screamed and waved our hands. Babette grabbed her puce sari from the rocks and ran through the sand with the gown streaming behind her. She looked like one of those Olympic dancers with the ribbons.

"I'm sure they saw us," said Ota Sato. "They'll be back."

Everyone walked excitedly back to the temple-prison. Babette and Mona were talking to each other like old friends. We seemed to have forgotten all about Bah's dead body back at the pit. While everyone was packing up their suitcases and bags, Abou came and sat down next to me.

"Finnegan," he said, "I have something strange to show you."

I followed him into the prison yard. Was he taking me to the pit? No, Abou turned toward the cell containing the phony Muhammad. Glancing behind him to make sure we were alone, he pulled the wooden door. To our surprise, it wouldn't open.

"The lock is too old," he said. "How could—" And then we saw it. I mean, we saw them. The pair of handcuffs that Ota Sato had brought with him on the bus. The pair that the other writers took turns trying to escape from. One iron cuff was fastened to the inner doorknob, and the other was looped around the rusty lock piece that fastened to the door jamb.

"These were not here yesterday afternoon," said Abou. He pulled on the door as far as it would reach. "Finnegan, can you see Muhammad?"

"It's not Muhammad."

"Whoever he is! Can you still see him?"

I pushed my head in the narrow space between the door and the jamb. Once again, I could see the shape of the mysterious corpse beneath the ancient Legionnaire blanket.

"Do you think you can squeeze in there?" said Abou.

"Are you crazy?" I said.

"Please, Finnegan. It's important."

"What if I get locked inside?"

"If you can get in, you can get out."

"No, thanks." I'd had enough of being trapped in dark rooms and tunnels.

"This may be a matter of life and death," said Abou. "And it may help us discover what happened to your uncle."

I squeezed into the cell. The room didn't smell quite as bad as I thought it would, but it was still bad. I thought I was going to throw up.

"Go look at the feet," said Abou.

"We already did that," I said.

"Look at the feet."

I don't know what had gotten into Abou, but to

humor him I walked over to the corpse and lifted up the end of the blanket.

"Well?"

I was stunned. "How did you know?" I said.

"A hunch. But let's go quickly, before we are discovered."

"How can this help Uncle Stop?" I asked, squeezing back through the entrance.

"I am not sure, Finnegan. But I know we're getting closer to solving this puzzle."

How could Abou have known? When I lifted up the blanket to see those cold, blue feet again, the feet were gone. The whole body was gone! A mound of straw had been lumped and padded into shape under the blanket to resemble a body.

Did the same person who shoved Omar Bah into the death pit also steal the fake Muhammad's body?

Questions bounced through my mind like pinballs. I left Abou behind me, still struggling to remove the handcuffs from the door. I walked slowly back to the men's quarters. The bald, crazy emperor still stared blankly down the hall. Soon he would be alone again.

Then I saw the second piece of paper. Crumpled up into a ball like the first one, small as a pencil eraser, it lay a few yards from the emperor's stony reddish feet. I quickly opened it and saw a scrap resembling the first one—thin white paper, black printing, bits and pieces of words. This time I could make out another complete word: RESTAURANT. Restaurant? The only restaurant I could think of was that fast-food joint back in Fuz where we had those soy-and-tofu burgers. Was someone trying to warn me about Burger Sheik's? Or was there a restaurant in Aznac that held some clue? Perhaps it was a code word. *Restaurant* might refer to our feast yesterday with Bletz's plane provisions or to the party last night.

Then I noticed something else. The letters *R* and *A* were heavily underscored, as if by a fingernail. By someone without a pencil? Letters in the other words or word sections were also underlined. A code! Back inside the men's room, I found a notebook and pencil among Uncle Stoppard's things and began copying down the underlined letters from left to right, top to bottom. I was right. It was a code. The letters spelled out a single, unbelievable sentence:

Ravenwood is dead.

I sat down on the sandstone floor with a bump. Truman Ravenwood, the founder of the Ruby Raven award, was dead? How could anyone here in the Temple know that? Ravenwood was in Aznac.

Was the message a warning? A warning that Ravenwood would soon be dead if certain precautions were not taken?

I glanced at the scrap of paper. Restaurant. Pieces of other words. Wait! The words were in French. French was the second official language of Occo. Uncle Stoppard had said that all the Sahara countries spoke it. That's why he didn't buy the Fuzi dictionary back at the airport giftshop. Uncle Stop said the French dictionary he had bought in Paris would be enough for—

The dictionary! This thin scrap of paper, like the other one with the word RENDEZVOUS, were from Uncle Stoppard's dictionary. He was communicating with me.

Uncle Stoppard was alive!

But where? I spun around and stared at the dark corners of the empty men's chamber. Was Uncle Stoppard hiding from the killer, as Abou had suspected? Or was he trapped somewhere without food and water? But how did he get this paper in the hallway? Was Uncle

Stoppard sneaking around the temple-prison during the night, dropping clues like bread crumbs? If that was the case, he should have dropped them on my cot. Or in my shoes.

I ran to the door of the men's chamber and stuck my head into the hall. No one. Only the bald emperor and the painted hero fighting the painted bull.

My list of questions was growing longer and longer. I closed my fist around that tiny scrap of paper. I could barely feel it, but it proved that Uncle Stoppard was alive. But for how long? Was he growing weak from a lack of food and water? And how did Uncle Stoppard know that Truman Ravenwood was dead? Carefully, I folded up the scrap and shoved it in my pocket. I needed to tell Abou the terrific news about Uncle Stop's clues.

Abou was standing outside with the others near the entrance to the temple-prison. Several Land Rovers were arriving at the foot of the temple steps. Dark men in chocolate uniforms, red berets, and mirror sunglasses jumped out and greeted us. One man, with gold braid on his left shoulder, and a short, military-looking mustache, introduced himself as Captain Dhawq of the Aznac Desert Guard.

"The Ruby Raven party, I presume," he said.

"Some party," said Mona. "Are you taking us to Aznac?"

"Shortly, Madame," said the captain. "We also have a small plane to search for."

"That's me," said Bletz. He bounced down the steps and shook the captain's hand. "My plane was forced down about a mile from here."

"You are the Russian pilot from Fuz?"

"Yes, sir," said Bletz. "Not originally from Fuz, of course."

"Fuz or no Fuz, it does not matter. We shall sort it out later. Do you need medical assistance?" The captain was looking at Bletz's sling.

"It's just a sprain," said Bletz.

Captain Dhawq looked at our group approvingly. "You seem to have survived the sandstorm and the desert admirably well. For writers."

"Not all of us survived," said Ota Sato. But Uncle Stoppard survived, I thought to myself. The ex-sumo wrestler told Captain Dhawq everything that had happened to us since our bus had been caught in the sandstorm. Captain Dhawq listened in amazement, his dark eyebrows performing gymnastic maneuvers. The other Desert Guards exchanged looks of disbelief. When Ota finished his recital, the captain said, "To sum up, your bus driver and, uh, Monsieur Omar Bah both met with fatal accidents?"

"Correct," said Ota Sato.

"Excuse me, sir," said Abou. "But identification has not been confirmed on the body."

"What about his birthmark?" said Babette.

"Yeah, the birthmark on his foot," added Mona.

"It's gone," I said.

"The man's foot is gone?" asked the captain.

"No, his head is gone," said Babette.

"And his birthmark," Abou said.

"The birthmark was on his head?" asked the captain.

"The birthmark was on his foot," I said. "And that's gone."

Captain Dhawq blew his whistle. "Foot or no foot, we shall sort all this out back in Aznac. Take us to the bodies."

Ota Sato led Captain Dhawq, followed by our group and several of the Desert Guards, into the prison yard. Captain Dhawq and his men stared at the guillotine. We walked over to the pit.

"There," Sato pointed.

"I cannot believe it," said Captain Dhawq.

"I know," Babette said. "Last night, we were talking with him and this morning—"

"No," said the captain. "That is not what I meant. I mean that I do not believe that Omar Bah is lying at the bottom of that pit."

"There's his beard," I said. "And that green thing is his fooz."

"Fooz or no fooz, that body down there does not belong to Omar Bah," said Captain Dhawq. "One hour ago, I left Monsieur Bah very much alive back in Aznac."

12

Aznac

Omar Bah was alive?

We all stood stunned by the news until Captain Dhawq ordered, "Take me to the other body." Ota Sato led the way to the cell containing the phony bus driver's body.

"This door won't open," said Ota Sato.

"What are these handcuffs doing here?" demanded Captain Dhawq.

"Um, I think they're mine, sir," said Sato, puzzled.

The captain turned to one of his uniformed men. "Fatah, break down the door."

The brawnier of the two Desert Guards simply nodded.

"Don't you have a key?" asked Abou.

The wooden door burst inward under Fatah's lunging assault.

"Why would I have a key to that door?" said the captain.

"I meant a handcuff key," said Abou.

"Of course," said Captain Dhawq. He turned to the second, smaller guardsman and said, "Keys." The second guardsman handed him a pair from his utility belt. Then Captain Dhawq walked over to the remnants of the shattered door and unlocked the cuffs that hung from the jamb. He gave the cuffs to Fatah and said, "Put these on that gentleman." He pointed to Abou.

"You can't!" I shouted.

Captain Dhawq looked sternly at Abou while Fatah handcuffed him. "How do you know so much more about the dead bus driver than your friends?"

Abou looked scared.

"Who is the dead body inside this room?" demanded the captain.

"Our bus driver, Muhammad," said Babette.

"No, it's not," said Abou.

"Who is it?" asked the captain.

Abou looked down at his stockinged feet. "I'm not sure."

"Captain," said Fatah, grimly. The huge guard whipped the blanket off the cot, revealing the mound of straw in the shape of a body. Ota Sato yelled something in Japanese.

"He's gone," said Babette.

"Your bus driver?" said Captain Dhawq.

"He was lying right there," said Mona. "We all saw Bah and Sato drag him in here."

"It was not Muhammad," said Abou, struggling against the cuffs.

"Then tell me who it was," said the captain.

"I told you, I'm not sure yet."

"Perhaps you will know once you are sitting in the jail in Aznac."

"You can't put him in jail," I cried. "His mother is a princess."

"A princess?" said the captain.

"Yeah, she's Lily Oblong."

"That's Lallah Oolah," said Abou.

"Of Burger Sheik's?" said the smaller guard. "I love her pomegranate shakes."

"Shakes or no shakes, we'll sort this all out in Aznac," said the captain. He snapped some orders to the two guards concerning Abou, and sent for two other guards who waited outside to come and fetch the body from the bottom of the bone pit. More guards hustled us, luggage and all, into one of the Land Rovers.

"I can't go," I said. "My uncle is still here."

"The bodies will all be brought back to Aznac," said Captain Dhawq.

"He's not a body. He's still alive."

"Into the vehicle."

"I have to stay! Please!"

Two guards lifted me and pushed me into the Land Rover. "Do not force us to use handcuffs on you, too, young man," called the captain.

"Please!" I cried.

"We will talk in Aznac," said the captain.

"What will happen to Abou?"

"Do not worry about him," said Captain Dhawq. He slammed the door shut and gave an order to the driver. We rolled out of the canyon in a cloud of orange dust. I gave the prison one last backward look. Now that I was sure Uncle Stoppard was still alive, I was being forced to abandon him. Now who would read his clues? Once the Desert Guards left Mortville, Uncle Stoppard would be completely alone. Alone with the ghosts and the cobras and the guillotine.

I felt alone, too. Abandoned. I was on my way to a strange city, surrounded by strangers. No parents, no uncle, no Abou.

"I'm sure Abou will join us in Aznac," Babette said, patting my shoulders with her plump, warm hands, trying to be cheerful.

"But Uncle Stoppard—"

"This is more like it," said Mona. "Air conditioning, comfortable seats, and ashtrays."

Nada Kloo bent over to me and whispered. "Why

doesn't your friend think the dead body belongs to Muhammad?"

"The stupid birthmark," I said, wiping my eyes on my arm. I explained my discovery of the backwards C. I told how Abou had wiped the ink off the corpse's foot with his handkerchief.

"You're rather observant, Finn," said Babette, pulling out her purple notepad. "I must use that clue in my next book."

"Is the body . . . Mr. Sterling?" asked Bletz.

"No, 'cause the rest of the body doesn't look like him." Thank goodness Uncle Stoppard has freckles.

"You're sure?" said Mona.

"I'm sure," I said. I didn't want to tell them that the body couldn't possibly belong to Uncle Stoppard, since Uncle Stoppard was still alive. I was worried that one of my fellow passengers might be the killer.

"That's a relief," said Babette.

"Who do you suppose the body is?" asked Ota Sato.

"I know who it is," said Mona, slyly. "And I was right all the time."

"Yeah? Who is it, Miss Squeer?" said Bletz.

"That's Trafalgar-Squeer. And isn't it obvious? The body is"—puff—"Brentano Zamboni."

Everyone gasped. Including our driver.

"How did he get here?" asked Babette.

"He was here all the time," said Mona. "He was probably hidden somewhere on the bus. Maybe on the roof, under that tarp up there. I told you, he and Wrong-Way Muhammad were in on it together."

"Zamboni hid on the bus and followed us to the prison?" Ota Sato didn't sound convinced.

"When Kloo led us through the sandstorm," said Mona, "who was the last person in line?"

"Muhammad," I said.

"That's why he carried my overnight bag with his free hand," said Babette.

"Free hand? Ha! His free hand was holding on to Zamboni. And Zamboni"—puff—"probably carried your bag, Babs. Then when we got to the mouth of the canyon, Zamboni dropped out of line and hid outside."

"It's too fantastic," said Ota Sato.

That's what Uncle Stoppard always said about Mona's plots.

"No more fantastic than having three candidates for the Ruby Raven eliminated under mysterious circumstances: Neez, Sterling, and Bah. The only other person who could possibly benefit from the Ravenwood money besides ourselves," said Mona, "is Zamboni. Zamboni and his accomplice got into a fight, there was a struggle, and the so-called Muhammad killed Zamboni."

"You think Muhammad is the murderer?" Kloo whispered.

"If Muhammad is his real name. Zamboni must have hired him back in Fuz."

Bletz looked skeptical. "Why the fake birthmark, Ms. Trafalgar-Squeer?"

"Simple," she said. "Muhammad realized he would be found out. Once Zamboni's body was discovered in the morning, we would figure out the killer had to be Muhammad, because how else would Zamboni get to Mortville through a sandstorm without help from someone? Sato, you said yourself that you can't plan a sandstorm. And you can't plan on your bus tipping over, or on ending up in some forgotten French Foreign Legion outpost. Zamboni must have been with us the whole time on the bus. And the most obvious person to help conceal him would be the bus driver, Muhammad."

Mona was looking pleased with herself. Babette was furiously taking notes.

"Therefore," continued the Queen of Crime, "in order to hide the fact that it was Zamboni's body and trick us into believing it was his own body, Muhammad sliced off Brentano's head—"

"Please!" Nada said.

"—and then he drew that phony birthmark on the sole of Zamboni's foot. But he made a stupid mistake."

"Did you know that Muslims never show the soles of their shoes or feet to anyone?" I said. No one paid any attention to me. They were all busy arguing with Mona.

"If you are so convinced," Babette said, "that we have been plagued by murders and not by mere misfortune, why don't you also believe that a stranger might be behind all this?" She darted a frightened look at Alexander Bletz.

"A stranger? Think, Babs! No one else knows about the award ceremony, or where we are. Only Raven-wood and"—puff—"the recipients of Ravenwood's telegram."

The yellow telegram in Minneapolis.

"What would a stranger gain," asked Mona, "from the deaths of a few mystery writers?"

"Revenge," suggested Ota Sato.

"Revenge?" asked the bewildered Kloo.

"So, where is Muhammad now, Mona?" asked Bletz.

"Mortville? Aznac? Who knows? If Sterling were here, he would say that the killer is disguised as our driver." I glanced up at the driver's mirror sunglasses reflected in the Rover's rearview mirror. "But I'm sure"—puff—"that he'll show up. Sterling, that is."

Mona's theory about the killer was interesting, but it didn't explain why the body of the fake Muhammad had been removed. Or who had removed it. And if Muhammad was indeed the killer, why would he push Omar

Bah into the pit? Wait, it wasn't Omar Bah according to Captain Dhawq.

Uncle Stoppard was missing. Brentano Zamboni was missing. "Muhammad's" body was missing. A head was missing. Omar Bah was dead. I mean, not Omar Bah. Who was really dead?

We arrived in Aznac an hour later. The ancient city is built on the ruins of a thousand-year-old Roman colony. Forests of white, sun-bleached pillars pop up everywhere between the red brick buildings built centuries later by the Arabs. Palm trees and date trees line the narrow streets. Our Land Rover rumbled through an older section of the city. Ancient Roman walls pressed in on either side of the road. For several miles we didn't see anything except for those walls. We slowed down in a cobbled courtyard. A spooky-looking mansion glowered at one end of the courtyard, with pillars, towers, and dozens of dark windows. At the foot of the mansion's front steps stood a suntanned man with spiky blond hair, earrings, and a long khaki overcoat. He waved when the Land Rover came into view.

"Madre de Dios!" exclaimed Babette. "It's Brentano Zamboni!"

Truman Ravenwood named his house Dead End. In Arabic it was called Tariq Masdood (it rhymes with "the geek was nude"). Ravenwood had moved to Aznac because of its association with Edgar Allan Poe, and there he fell in love with the Roman ruins and the winding, maze-like streets (which reminded him of mystery stories). Ravenwood then converted to Islam and built a house. With all his millions you'd think he could have built a cheerier-looking place. Ravenwood lived all alone except for a few servants, a black cat, and his personal assistant, the tiny Mr. Hyde. I learned all this from

Brentano Zamboni while he led us into the vast and gloomy mansion.

The thick barrier of bushes and trees surrounding Tariq Masdood turned the bright afternoon sunlight into shadowy dusk. A sound I hadn't heard since Uncle Stoppard and I left home greeted us as we filed out of the Rover. Crickets, thousands of them. It made me realize how silent and lifeless the Mortville prison had been. The cricket rattles penetrated the walls of Tariq Masdood as Zamboni escorted us along murky, carpeted corridors and into a large room stuffed with uncomfortable-looking furniture, greasy paintings on the walls, and blood-red curtains.

He closed the door. "Before Mr. Hyde gets here," he said, "I must tell you about Nabi Neez."

"We already know," said Mona.

"I saw it happen," said Babette.

"So did I," said Zamboni. "I was there, too, remember?"

"What exactly happened to you?" Babette asked.

Zamboni had slipped off his long khaki overcoat. Underneath he was wearing gray baggy pants, a white shirt, and a bright tie with a pelican painted on it. He nervously rubbed one of his earrings. "I was on the upper levels of the Mallomars . . ."

"Wait a moment," said Ota Sato. "We heard that Omar Bah isn't dead."

Zamboni laughed. "Why would he be dead?"

"Let Brentano finish his story," said Babette.

Zamboni took a deep breath. "At the Mallomars, I'd been looking around, taking pictures, and then I saw some guy at the far end of one of the tomb roofs. He was standing next to a fallen pillar. I thought it would make an interesting shot. I looked at him through the camera lens—it's got a telephoto attachment—when I suddenly realized he was pushing the pillar! I yelled at him, but he must not have heard me. I ran over to stop him—"

Zamboni's footsteps were the ones I heard that day.

"—it was too late. The pillar disappeared over the edge of the roof. I heard a terrific crash. I looked over the edge and could see you, Babette, and Stoppard, and some legs sticking out from under the pillar. I recognized Nabi's new shoes."

"Those damn shoes!" Babette said. "If only the laces hadn't come loose, and he hadn't stopped to tie them."

Mona had lit another cigarette. "So you were by the pillar," she said.

"I stood there for a few seconds," said Brentano. "I guess I was in shock. Then I realized the other guy was still there too. He was looking down at the mess, muttering to himself. He seemed terrifically angry about something."

"Was he wearing an orange robe?" I asked.

Zamboni looked at me for the first time. "An orange djellabah, yes. Who are you?"

"This is Stoppard's nephew," said Babette. "Finnegan Zwake."

"Zwake?"

"Like the explorers, you know."

"Where is Stoppard?" said Zamboni. "Is he joining us later?"

"It's a long story," said Mona. "Perhaps you better finish telling us what happened."

Zamboni rubbed his earring. "This other guy—the one in the orange djellabah—finally realized I was there. And then I realized that he realized I was there. We must have stared at each other for thirty seconds."

"Did you get a good look at him?" asked Ota Sato.

"No, because of the hood. Most of his face was in shadow."

"Convenient," Mona said.

Zamboni shot a quick glance at Mona, then continued. "The guy stared at the camera round my neck. He must have thought that I had taken a picture of him pushing the pillar, catching him in the act. He growled and leaped at me. Actually growled! I was caught completely off guard. He kept tugging at the camera, and I kept trying to pull away from him. We fought for several minutes up there on the roof. Then he pushed me backwards. I felt myself falling and then—nothing. I blacked out. When I came to, it was dark out. I could see stars. I mean, *real* stars."

"Heavens!" exclaimed Babette.

"My camera was missing. And there was blood in my hair. I guess I must have hit my head when that fellow pushed me and I lost consciousness for a few hours. I headed back toward the parking lot with a splitting headache. Then I saw something on the roof, something white, close to the place where that guy and I had been struggling with the camera. It was this." Brentano reached into a pocket of his gray baggy pants and pulled out a thin white cylinder.

"A cigarette?" Bletz said.

"A British cigarette," said Brentano. "To be precise, a Silk Cut, that's the brand name. You can see the pale lavender printing next to the filter."

I smelled a rich mixture of hay and mint ice cream.

"British cigarette?" Babette said. "How extremely interesting."

Everyone in the room turned to look at Mona. She sat on a blood-red velvet sofa, nervously playing with the tassels of a small pillow. I had never seen the Queen of Crime nervous before. She slowly stood up.

"You honestly believe I had something to do with Nabi's death?" Mona said, looking around at her accusers.

"You were the one casting suspicions on Brentano," said Babette.

"I suppose you think I killed Muhammad, too?"

"You were the person who found the body," said Babette.

"This is utterly"—puff— "ridiculous. When that pillar was hurtling through the air toward Nabi—and unfortunately missed one of his companions—I was having lunch at the Hôtel Splendide restaurant. I have a witness. A reporter from *Peephole* magazine."

I thought Abou was from *Peephole*. Was anyone telling the truth?

Mona stood up and walked toward the fireplace. "Where is Ravenwood?" she demanded. "All these accusations are wasting time. We need to get on with the award ceremony."

"How did your cigarette end up in the Mallomar tombs, Mona?" said Nada Kloo.

"It's a British cigarette!" Mona said. "I'm not the only one who smokes them. All of Britain smokes them!"

Ota Sato turned toward Zamboni. "You never told us how *you* got here."

"I walked to the highway," said Zamboni, "and thumbed a ride back to the hotel. The place was humming with police. They found a dead body in the lobby."

"Potted in the palms," said Nada Kloo, nodding.

Brentano gulped. "You were there?"

"Long enough to discover the bus had preceded us to Aznac," said Kloo. "And how did you get here?"

"First, I told the police what I had seen up at Mallomar. Then I took a bus the following morning and avoided the sandstorm. I've been here two days now."

"And the award ceremony?" asked Babette.

A squeaky, nasal voice answered, "It's been postponed."

We all turned around and saw little Mr. Hyde standing at the opposite end of the room. His pale blue suit was replaced by a mournful black one. "Only natural under the circumstances to postpone it," he said.

"Listen, Hyde," said Mona. She threw her cigarette into the fireplace and took a few steps toward the little man. "We heard that Omar Bah is here in Aznac."

Hyde smiled a crooked smile. "Yes, he's right here in Tariq Masdood."

"But he fell," said Kloo hoarsely.

"I saw his green fooz at the bottom of the bone pit," I said.

"Bone pit?" Brentano sat down on a plump green footstool. "What are you all talking about? And why do you think Omar Bah is dead?"

For the second time that day, Ota Sato explained what had happened to us during the sandstorm and at the abandoned prison. By this time, the sunlight outside the windows was gone and the crickets were playing a full orchestra. Zamboni looked more amazed at Sato's story than Captain Dhawq had.

"You still don't know what happened to Stoppard?" he asked. "Hey, you had better talk to Omar. This is even *worse* news."

How could it be worse if Omar Bah was still alive?

Mr. Hyde walked over to the fireplace and pulled on a long sash that led up to the ceiling. A gong sounded somewhere in the mansion. A pair of doors opened and in swooped the magnificent figure of Omar Bah, mustache, gold spectacles, and green fooz intact. Babette fainted in her chair.

"I have been listening to your fantastic story from the next room," he said. "And I am extremely pleased to say that I am alive. Hyde, I believe Miss Lizardo requires some water." Bah beamed at his startled guests. "I also am afraid that the news of my continued breathing will serve to make matters worse."

"How could things be worse, Bah?" said Mona. "You're alive."

Bah nodded gravely. "And someone else is dead."

"Yes," I said. "Someone dressed up like you is lying at the bottom of the bone pit in Mortville prison."

"I'm afraid that man," said Omar Bah, "is none other than Truman Ravenwood."

13
Shakespeare

Ravenwood was dead. I felt for the piece of crumpled paper in my pocket. Its statement was true.

"Ravenwood disguised himself as me," said Omar Bah. "I knew all about it. I even gave him some of my clothes to wear. Then I decided to wait here while he played his silly practical joke and—"

There was a loud banging at the front doors. Zamboni started to move, but Bah touched his arm. "The servants will get it."

Babette shook her head, unbelieving. "That was Ravenwood back at the hotel?"

"That was Ravenwood on the bus?" said Mona.

Omar Bah's black beard bobbed up and down on his massive chest.

"Then that's Ravenwood in the bone pit," said Ota Sato.

"Ravenwood loved practical jokes," said Omar Bah. "And mysteries. That's why he put my name on the telegram list without a book title next to it. It was a clue that 'Omar Bah' was different from the other authors. For your information, I am not nominated for the Ruby Raven. Why should I be? I haven't published anything in years. But I was invited to be the master of cere- monies."

The door opened a second time. A solemn-looking

butler padded into the room. He walked up to me and held out a silver platter. A folded card rested on its gleaming surface. "For the young gentleman," he said. For me? Then he turned and walked out. The folded card turned out to be the front cover torn from a paperback, *The Case of the Cairo Gyro*. As the writers and Mr. Hyde continued discussing the tragic fate of Mr. Ravenwood, I quietly slipped out the door.

Abou stood in a dim shadow of the hallway, looking shoeless and afraid.

"Finnegan, you must help me."

"What's going on? Did the police bring you here?"

"In a manner of speaking. Their Land Rover brought me here. But, um, they're still stuck back at the prison."

"Abou!"

"I had to. They were going to lock me up here in Aznac. Do you know what an Occan jail is like? It's not pretty. It might be months before they let me see my mother."

"But how did you escape?"

"Sato's been experimenting with those cuffs for months. And I'm sure my pulling on them when they were attached to the cell door must have helped loosen them. As soon as I started struggling with them, they began to unhinge. Let's get out of the hall, in case one of the writers comes out looking for you."

We sneaked through a door at the end of the gloomy corridor.

The room we entered was lit by a thousand candles. A long table of dark polished wood lay in the center of the room, with eight chairs on either side. China plates, crystal goblets, silver knives and forks gleamed silently. "This must be for the banquet," I whispered.

At the head of the table stood a tall pedestal draped in snowy fabric. And on top of the pedestal sat the dark and glittering reason for Uncle Stoppard's and my traveling thousands of miles and ending up in this horrible place. The Ruby Raven.

"Wow!" exclaimed Abou.

Sleek black feathers were carved in the statue's side. Its evil-looking beak was sharp as a cobra's fang. Ruby eyes glittered in its ink-black head, and a larger ruby hung on a gold pendant round its neck. The black bird was only a foot high, but it seemed immense. Like a black hole in outer space, a tiny point in the universe with gravity so powerful that nothing can resist it, the Ruby Raven had drawn people from all over the globe to this one spot in the middle of the Sahara Desert. Drawn them here, or destroyed them along the way.

Was this piece of plaster and jewelry worth a human life? Who would kill in order to have this black knick-knack sitting on their coffee table?

I don't know how long I had been staring at the Raven, when Abou touched my shoulder and snapped me out of the bird's spell.

"I'm sure the police are looking for me," Abou said. "And this will be one of the first places they look. Will you go with me?"

"Go? Where?"

"I have an aunt who lives here in Aznac. Lalla Rimah. I'm sure she'll let us stay with her."

"But, Abou—"

"We must hurry. The police could arrive any minute."

"What about Uncle Stoppard? I thought you were going to help me find him."

Abou's warm brown eyes blinked at me from behind his yellow-framed glasses.

"I have another question, Abou. Mona said she had an interview with a *Peephole* reporter. But you said that you were the reporter."

Abou swallowed hard. "I know. My editor told me to stay and cover the airport bombings while he sent another reporter to cover the awards. I only said all that so I'd get a chance to meet Stoppard Sterling. I'm his biggest fan, you know."

"And now you have to help him."

Abou stared at the Ruby Raven. "Yes, you are right. But I need to hide, Finn."

"Wait here."

I slipped quietly out of the banquet room and found one of Ravenwood's servants roaming the halls. I asked to be shown to the room reserved for Stoppard Sterling. The servant led me back upstairs. Abou silently trailed us, concealed by the shadows in the gloomy hallways. He followed the servant and me up to the third floor, where I was shown into a huge blue and yellow bedroom with antique furniture and a blazing fireplace. As soon as the servant left, Abou slipped inside and closed the door.

"Do the police think you killed Muhammad?" I asked. "Or whoever he is."

"They think I had something to do with it," Abou said. "If I had only kept my big mouth shut about that missing birthmark, and about the body's being the wrong one . . ."

"Now what do we do?"

"I guess we figure out who the real killer is before the police get here."

"We don't have enough time!"

"It will have to be enough. I'm sure we have all the information. Let's calm down and be logical about all of this."

"Like the Scientific Detective," I said.

"Yes, like the S.D."

There were so many questions on our list. How do we start?

First off, I surprised Abou with the news that Omar Bah and Brentano Zamboni were both alive and that Truman Ravenwood was dead. I was saving the best news for last.

"That was Ravenwood dressed up as Bah? I thought he was from England. How did he know all that stuff about Occo and the desert?"

"Ravenwood's lived here for the past two years," I said. "And Brentano Zamboni said that he converted to Islam. And speaking of Zamboni . . ." I recounted the Italian's adventures back at Mallomar. I mentioned the British cigarette he found after fighting with the man in the orange hood.

"British, huh?"

Brentano's cigarette reminded me of my own small discovery. I pulled the crumpled paper from my pocket. "Look at this." Abou took the paper and unfolded it.

"Restaurant?" He gave me a puzzled look.

"The other side."

Abou flipped the scrap over and stared.

"You found this back at the Temple?" he said.

"Yes, before any of us knew about Ravenwood."

"But who—?"

"Uncle Stoppard is alive!" I said. I explained the French dictionary that Uncle Stop brought with him from Paris. "I'm sure Uncle Stoppard figured no one else would figure out what those scraps from a dictionary would mean. Only I would understand."

"That's terrific, Finn!"

"Here's another one he sent me." I showed Abou the scrap with the word RENDEZVOUS.

"Ha, both *R* words."

R words?

"Rose!" I shouted. "Abou, I forgot to tell you."

We heard voices in the hall. Abou jumped up and

quickly hid behind the drapes. I went to the door and peered out. It was Mona and the others. The servants were showing all the writers to their various rooms.

"Tonight I shall sleep like a log," said Babette.

"Those cots were impossible," said Mona. "And last night, someone kept talking in his sleep."

"You heard that, too?" Babette asked. "It was more irritating than Kloo's snoring." They each vanished into a bedroom. I closed the door and walked over to the drapes. Abou was gone!

"Abou!"

His head popped out from under the bed.

"It's only the writers," I said.

"I guess I'm a bit jumpy."

"People are getting ready for dinner," I said. I hoped it wasn't baked polar bear.

Abou climbed out from his hiding place, and I told him about the mysterious voice I had heard in the night. The voice that kept whispering about roses and blurs and sand. The voice that didn't sound like anyone from the bus, a stranger's voice.

"Do you think it's important?" I asked.

"Yes, because it's a voice you didn't recognize. If Muhammad was in disguise, perhaps his voice was disguised, too."

"It could have been Ravenwood," I said. "In his real voice."

"Hmm, that's one possibility," Abou said. "What exactly did the voice say? Try to remember it word for word, if you can."

Uncle Stoppard says I have a phenomenal memory, especially for remembering sounds and conversations. I guess it's good, but I don't always remember the stuff that I would like to. I concentrated and thought back to our first night in the prison. I tried to imagine the circle of cots, the faint embers of our campfire, the incredible darkness of that cold stone room.

"Something about a blur," I said.

"A blur?"

"And then, 'Toss over the slinky sand a rose.'"

"What? Did you say arrows?"

"No, not arrows. A rose. Though I guess it does sound like arrows."

Abou's face lit up. "Finnegan. I think this is it! Listen to me. What am I saying?"

I listened and then said, "You repeated what I said. 'Toss over the slinky sand a rose.'"

"No, no. What I said was: 'To suffer the slings and arrows.' But you heard something else. If you aren't sure what it is I'm saying, if you don't see it written down, you might get confused and hear something else. For instance, I could say a story was *no bull*. But you might hear me say it was *noble*."

"Slings and arrows. I've heard that before."

"Of course, you have," said Abou. "'To suffer the slings and arrows of outrageous fortune.'"

"A rose of outer ages. That's what I heard!"

"You heard part of 'arrows of outrageous fortune.' You only thought you heard 'a rose of outer ages.'"

"What is it?"

"Shakespeare," said Abou. "It's from *Hamlet*. From Hamlet's most famous speech. 'To be or not to be, that is the question, whether 'tis nobler'—"

"Nobler," I shouted. "No blur! That's what I heard."

"Keep it down. We don't want the others to hear you."

"*Hamlet*. Like Uncle Stoppard's book."

"Exactly," said Abou. "Someone was reciting Shakespeare."

"In his sleep?"

"Someone in disguise, who had changed his—or her—voice, who carried wigs with him on the bus, someone who kept changing his identity like a chameleon, so easily and quickly that we couldn't keep track. Let's look at that list again, Finnegan."

Abou pulled out his list from his pocket.

1. Where is Uncle Stoppard?
2. Who was killed last night? (or, same question, Who was Muhammad?)
3. Who was killed at the hotel? (Zamboni?)
4. Who was the person Finn heard running in the Mallomar Tombs?
5. Who brought the wigs and why?
6. Why wasn't a title listed next to Omar Bah's name on the telegram?
7. If he's not dead, what happened to Brentano Zamboni?
8. Who stole the blank pages from Mona's notebook and why?
9. Who is Alexander?
10. Who was the guy in the Orange Hood at Mallomar?
11. How did Omar Bah know the word "yucky"?

"Well, we know the answers to 4, 6, and 7," I said.

"And 10," said Abou. "Hmm, when you and I discovered the phony birthmark back at the Temple, we wondered who the dead body belonged to. It wasn't your uncle's, and we knew there couldn't simply be an extra body lying around. And then after Omar Bah died—"

"Ravenwood," I said.

"That's right, after Ravenwood, disguised as Omar Bah, died. Hey, wait a minute! Bats."

"Yucky bats?" I asked.

"Yucky bats," said Abou. "If Ravenwood was disguised as Bah, how would he know about the bats? Ravenwood wasn't at Mallomar."

"The killer was at Mallomar," I said.

"And the killer was not Ravenwood," said Abou. "Therefore the killer was not the fake Omar Bah."

"But the fake Omar Bah knew about the word *yucky*," I said.

Abou started jumping around. "So that's why there wasn't a body under the blanket!"

"Why?"

"Don't you see, Finnegan? The killer exchanged bodies."

"Exchanged?"

"Like that scary movie about the body snitchers."

"Body snatchers."

"That's the one. First, the killer was disguised as Muhammad, a fake Muslim. Omar Bah/Ravenwood must have figured out he was a phony."

I remembered the expression on Omar Bah's, I mean, Ravenwood's face, as he almost collided with me in the hallway that first night back in Mortville. He had been staring at me while I helped our bus driver off with his shoes. Ravenwood suspected something then. He knew that no true Muslim would expose the bottom of his foot to a perfect stranger like me. And Ravenwood knew all the traditions of Islam, since he had recently converted. That's what Bah/Ravenwood meant by the word *soul*. He was talking about the *sole* of the foot, not the *soul* inside your body. I had confused those words, just as I had confused Hamlet's words. If only I had read more Shakespeare in school, or in the library with Uncle Stoppard. I would have been able to figure out what the whisperer back in Mortville was saying. Maybe I could have prevented Uncle Stoppard from disappearing. From now on, I'm spending more time at the library.

"The snatcher is still with us," said Abou.

"Here in Tariq Masdood?" I said.

"The killer was probably right there in the Rover when you drove here."

Those sunglasses reflected in the rearview mirror.

"But who—? Of course! There is only one person it can be," said Abou.

"Who?" I said.

"Think of it, Finnegan. Disguises. Come on!" He grabbed me by the hand and pulled me out the door.

"But the police—" I said.

"Who cares?" Abou said. "They'll listen to me now."

Abou knocked on doors up and down the hall while my head was spinning with clues. Disguises, different voices, wigs, the poison dart, the cobra in the bathroom, the mail. Of course! Mail. All that mail.

Ota Sato opened the first door. "Abou? What are you doing here? What did the police have to say?"

"You will be joining us for dinner, won't you, Sato?" Abou said.

"Of course, I will. What do—?"

"Where is Miss Kloo?" asked Abou.

Sato pointed across the hall. "I believe that's her room."

Abou knocked. Bletz answered the door.

"Yes?" said the Russian pilot.

"Miss Kloo, please," said Abou.

"She's washing up for dinner," said Bletz. Nada Kloo appeared through a door at the far end of the bedroom, delicately adjusting her white veil and gloves.

"Miss Kloo," said Abou. There was something different in Abou's tone. He sounded smooth and oily. "Please forgive me, Miss Kloo, but I've been asked to make a request. We all understand you are allergic to sunlight, and Ravenwood's household uses only candles. Mr. Hyde thought it would be an honor if you would, well . . . unveil yourself to us at dinner tonight."

"Of course," said Kloo. "It's such a habit of mine to wear this. I'll take it off right after the ceremony."

"Why not now?" I said.

"Well—"

"Yes, why not, Nada darling?" said Alexander. "I want everyone to see how gorgeous you are."

She laughed. "Alexy, can't it wait?"

"You look delectable by candlelight," said Bletz.

Nada stared at him. I mean, I guess she stared. I couldn't see her face through the gauzy white veil.

"This is terribly flattering," she said. "Now I'll have to fix my hair. I'll see you gentlemen downstairs at dinner." She waved her fingers at us and slipped back into the washroom.

"Mr. Bletz, do you still have your gun?" said Abou.

Alexander patted the breast of his padded jacket. "I always keep it. Ever since the war in Afghanistan. I guess it's become a habit, like Nada's veil."

"We may need it sometime during dinner," Abou said.

"Dinner?" asked the pilot.

"We know who killed Nabi Neez," I said. "And our bus driver."

"You know who the killer is?"

Abou smiled. "The killer will be dining with us, Mr. Bletz. I came over here to ask about your gun and—"

We heard the sound of breaking glass. It came from the washroom.

"Nada?" cried Bletz. He rushed into the washroom and then ran back out. "She's gone!" he said. Abou and I ran into the washroom. It was empty. Silky curtains flapped beside a large hole in the window. Gauzy white strands of fabric fluttered from jagged spikes of glass. I peered through the window. "She's down there." A small white figure was running among the dark palm trees.

"The courtyard," said Abou.

The three of us raced down the hall toward the stairs. Mona stuck her head out a door. "What on earth is going on?" she said.

"Nada Kloo," I said.

"Well then, who *does* have a clue?" Mona followed us down the two flights of stairs. Mr. Hyde joined us on the front steps of the mansion.

"What is all this noise?" he demanded.

"Where did she go?" asked Bletz, searching for signs of his beloved mummy.

The dark courtyard was deserted, except for the Land Rover that Abou had borrowed.

"Don't tell me the Desert Guard have returned already," Mona said, catching sight of the vehicle.

"It's empty," I said. "That's how Abou—"

The Land Rover started up and shot through the courtyard gates.

"It's her," said Alexander.

"How can we catch her?" I cried.

"The garage." Mr. Hyde pointed to the side of the mansion. "There might be something in there." The five of us ran to the garage. Mr. Hyde opened a side door and switched on a light. A huge black Bentley gleamed in the middle of the room. Two mopeds leaned by the door, one green and one blue.

"The servants use those for running errands," said Mr. Hyde.

"You have a key for the car?" asked Mona.

"Well, I'd have to go inside and then—"

All this chitchat was taking too long. The killer could

be miles away before the stupid car was ever started. The mopeds looked faster than the car, anyway. How do you turn it on? I guess the button that says "on," huh? I jumped on the green moped and in seconds I was cruising out of the courtyard.

"Finn!" Abou yelled behind me.

Only one road led away from Tariq Masdood, hemmed in on both sides by ancient Roman walls. If I was fast enough, I might catch up with Kloo before she reached the road's end and vanished down some slippery side street.

Too bad I was riding a moped instead of a Harley. At least I was moving forward.

Suddenly, the other moped pulled alongside of me. Bletz and Mona. The Russian's long blond hair streamed back into Mona's face. I think it was the only time I saw Mona without a cigarette.

Far up ahead, I could see the glimmer of red taillights. Bletz must have seen it, too. I slammed down on the accelerator and shot forward. I didn't think mopeds could go that fast, but I probably provided less wind resistance than the big, boxy Land Rover. There were some advantages to being smaller. Up ahead, the taillights grew brighter. I drew closer and closer to the fleeing Kloo. But now I could see that the end of the road was also approaching. Half a mile beyond the Rover stood the ancient stone gate that led into the road. As soon as she was through that gate, Kloo could drive anywhere. The Rover pulled away from us. She must have been doing close to ninety miles per hour. Or whatever that is in kilometers.

"We won't make it," Mona shouted from the other moped.

"Yes, we will," I shouted back.

"We won't make it!"

The Roman gate was narrower than the road. And

the Land Rover was wider than an average vehicle. A horrible crunch! The Rover's left front fender struck the stone gate. The car swung around with an ear-splitting screech, and its right side slammed into the opposite wall. Kloo crashed to a stop, blocking the road.

We pulled up and jumped off our mopeds. Bletz was the first one to reach the Rover. He yanked open the driver's door and shouted something. No one was inside. The door on the other side was open.

A black Bentley pulled up behind us. Abou jumped out. All four of us climbed quickly through the stalled Land Rover and into the street on the other side.

"There!" shouted Mona. A white figure was disappearing into what looked like another Roman ruin.

We followed the racing Bletz.

The Roman building was a great empty square shell, like an open garage. Walls rose up to meet a high, vaulted ceiling. Stars twinkled through small crevices in the stone. The back of the ruin seemed to be one vast, smooth wall unbroken by windows or doors. Fallen masonry littered the floor and slowed us in our search.

The white figure appeared next to the back wall.

"Stay away," Kloo shouted in a strange, husky voice.

"But Nada!" said Bletz.

"Stay away, I said." The figure lifted her arm toward us, exactly as she had lifted it in the sandstorm when the bus was lying on its side. This time, however, there was a gun in the mummy's hand.

Bletz pulled his jacket open and groped at his holster.

"She's taken my gun!" he said.

"And will use it," said the white figure. It was dark at the back of that huge room. It was hard to see anyone or anything clearly except for the ghostly figure in white. I thought she was aiming at me.

"I can't make him take back that abomination," said Kloo. "But I can take something from *him!*"

Him? She pointed the gun directly at me.

A shot rang out. The sound echoed through the ruin's shell, rumbling like thunder. The white figure was stained with a dark patch on its chest. It toppled backwards, shrieking.

Mona swung around. "Sato!" she cried.

Ota Sato was standing, not ten feet behind us, a smoking revolver at his side.

"Handcuffs are not the only thing I carry," he said.

Bletz had rushed forward. We found him, crouching behind a great block of stone, cradling Kloo's body in his big arms.

"Why? Why?" he said over and over. "Why was the money so important?"

Mona gently took Kloo's pulse. She looked at Abou and shook her head. Bletz wept over the lifeless body.

"I'm sorry," I said. "But I have to do this." I reached past Bletz and ripped off Kloo's white veil. Alexander Bletz almost dropped the body in surprise.

"Who is that?" he yelled.

Under the white hat and veil that Nada Kloo had worn since her arrival on the sand-swept road to Aznac, lay a pain-twisted face that did not belong to any female Russian novelist. It was the face of a dark-haired, blue-eyed, recently shaved man. Blood trickled from his nose. Abou fumbled under Kloo's blood-stained dress and drew out a small object.

"His passport?" said Mona.

Abou opened the document and read. "Mr. Sheridan Shakespeare of Avon, England."

"This is the man who drove our bus," I said.

"But Wittgenstein, no one's ever heard of this guy,"

said Mona. "What would he gain from killing off all the Raven nominees?"

"Nothing," said Abou.

"He wasn't after all the nominees," I said. "Only one."

"One?" Mona said.

"His eyes!" shouted Bletz. The Englishman's eyelids fluttered. "Where's Nada?" demanded the Russian. Bletz still held the dying figure in his arms. Now his arms threatened to break the figure in half. "Talk, you filthy creep, talk! What have you done with her?"

"Say something," I said.

The Englishman looked up at the Russian and smiled an evil smile. "Nada," he said.

Then Mr. Sheridan Shakespeare closed his eyes and died.

14
Secrets of the Temple

It was midnight when we returned to the prison of Mortville.

An ambulance had been summoned, and the Englishman's body had been taken away. The local police cleared the road, and a tow truck had hauled off the police Land Rover. Abou hid back at the mansion while Mona explained to the authorities she had no idea how the Rover came to be in the courtyard of Tariq Masdood. The dead man had probably—puff—stolen it. In the mansion, Abou explained to the unsmiling Mr. Hyde and the remainder of Truman Ravenwood's guests about the accident, the shooting and the unveiling of Mr. Shakespeare. I never knew adults could eat that fast, but after a rapid-fire dinner (while the police were clearing the road) the eight of us crammed into the shiny black Bentley and zoomed away from Aznac under a full moon. Mona was at the wheel.

No one talked much in the car during our trip. Abou handed me a list he had made during dinner. I made a few corrections and handed it back. We could read it by the small side-lights built into the cushioned walls next to the seat.

1. Poisoned dart
2. Mail bomb

3. Abou's yellow hat
4. Death of Muhammad
5. Disappearance of Stoppard Sterling
6. Clue of the Dictionary
7. Theft of Mona's notebook (blank pages)
8. Clue of the voice in the night
9. Pyramid bats
10. Why Omar Bah didn't tell a ghost story

I pondered the list all the way back to the Temple. The poisoned dart and the mail bomb. Why hadn't I been smarter? Because of my stupidity, Uncle Stoppard could be lying dead from starvation or heat exhaustion. Or cobra bites.

"Are cobra bites always fatal?" I asked Abou.

"No, they're not," said Babette from the front seat, next to Mona. "And I've done lots of research about snakes for my books. So I should know."

She and Mona shared a worried glance.

"There are the Teeth," said Ota. The full moonlight reflected off the desert sand and made it bright as Minnesota snow. Ahead of us, towering out of the glittering white sand, stood a familiar black wall of jagged stone.

"And there are the police," said Babette. At the base of the black cliffs, two sets of headlights gleamed toward us.

"They must have finally gotten someone to rescue them," said Ota Sato.

"Lucky them," said Abou with a gulp.

"They probably have walkie-talkies," I whispered to Abou. "Or cell phones."

"Hang on, people," said Mona. "Because I'm not stopping." She revved the accelerator and raced toward the oncoming lights. As the lights drew closer, we could see that they belonged to two more police Rovers.

Mona drove right between them. They swiftly whipped around in the sand and followed us.

"Careful, Miss Squeer," said Omar Bah. "This is not a race."

"Oh, yes it is!" she said.

"That's Trafalgar-Squeer," said Babette.

Mona reached the Teeth well before the Desert Guard. The Bentley plunged down the black canyon and hurtled past the iron Mortville gates. We skidded to a stop at the base of the steps. As we were climbing the stairs, the two Rovers drew up and flashed their headlights on us. A voice crackled through the canyon over a loudspeaker. "I command you to stop!" One of the Rover doors opened, and out stepped Captain Dhawq with his gold braid and red beret. He walked up the stairs and took hold of Abou's arm.

"I am placing you under arrest," he said. Other Desert Guards had disembarked, carrying black rifles.

"Wait, Captain Dhiwq," cried Mona.

"That's Dhawq," he said.

"Don't interrupt me," said Mona. "We are a rescue team of concerned international citizens and we are on a mission of life and death. Please allow us into the ruin, Captain. Give us just five minutes, and then you can arrest whomever you wish."

"This young man"—Captain Dhawq pointed at Abou—"is wanted for resisting arrest!"

"Five minutes, Captain," Mona said.

"But—"

"And then we'll explain why the Aznac police have the real murderer in a hospital morgue."

Captain Dhawq exploded. "Real murderer!"

"This way." Mona turned and led us up the steps and into the cold, stone hallway. This time, we had all brought flashlights from Tariq Masdood, courtesy of Mr.

Hyde. The hallway looked exactly as we had left it. There was the mad emperor between the two rooms. There was the crumbling painting of the hero and the bull.

Mona and Abou ran their hands along the surface of the painting.

"What are they doing?" shouted out Captain Dhawq.

"Uncle Stoppard," I shouted. "Where are you?"

"The inscription," said Abou. Below the painting ran an inscription carved into the stone:

IMPELLE UT PROSPERITATEM ATTINGAS

"Good thing they make us study Latin at Oxford," said Abou.

"What's it say?" asked Ota Sato.

"Press on and touch success," said Abou.

"How can four Latin words mean five American words?" I said.

Abou smiled, still running his hands along the wall. "Latin is different," he said. "With different forms."

Like Russian had a different alphabet.

"This one word *impelle* is a combination of two words, actually," he said. "Roughly meaning *press* and *on.*"

As I looked more closely at the ancient painting, I noticed small pencil-sized holes in the sandstone. They resembled the small holes in the other wall, the holes through which I and the murderer had spied on this wall from the tunnel. Holes large enough to shove a pencil through. Or a small crumpled piece of thin paper.

Press on. Press on. There must be a switch in this wall, like the one I touched in the tunnel. Mortville was probably crawling with secret passageways and hidden rooms.

Wait! I thought of the moped that I drove back in Aznac. How do you turn it on?

"Abou," I said. "Which word means on?"

"As I said, *impelle* combines the two words into one. But, if you want to be technical about it—"

"Yes, I do."

"Pelle means to strike or hit. And *im* means on."

I ran my fingers over the carved letters. "I M," I said. I pushed them, pressed *on. Press on and touch success.*

The bull split in two as the wall smoothly and quietly separated like the halves of a sliding door. A dark, forbidding gulf was revealed. Moonlight entered through a small opening set in the high ceiling. Wooden chairs and tables littered the room. Chains hung from the walls.

"Alexy!" came a small voice from the corner.

We pointed our flashlights toward the voice. The light from mine wobbled.

"Abou!" I shouted.

In the dark corner, looking tired and hungry, were two figures chained to the wall—a woman I had never seen before and Uncle Stoppard. I ran to my uncle and wrapped my arms around him. I didn't care how hard I squeezed. And I didn't care if anyone saw me crying.

"My little prince," he said.

"Who are these people?" shouted Captain Dhawq.

Mona introduced them to the captain, while his men released Nada Kloo (the *real* Nada Kloo) and Uncle Stoppard from their rusty chains.

"Stoppard Sterling?" Captain Dhawq's mustache quivered. "Not the Stoppard Sterling who wrote *Into My Grave?"*

Mona gave a disgusted look as Uncle Stoppard nodded weakly.

"Ah, yes, the great Shakespeare. The immortal Hamlet," said the captain.

"Begging your pardon, Captain," said Uncle Stoppard. "But I hope I never hear another line from Hamlet as long as I live. Which, for a while, I didn't think was going to be much longer. Could we please have some water?"

Nada Kloo put her arms around Bletz's neck. "Champagne, darling?" The Russian pilot winked and produced a bottle from his jacket. "Never mind the glasses," said Kloo. "I'm so thirsty I could chew off the cork."

The Desert Guard helped Nada and Uncle Stoppard out of the prison and sat them on the steps. They brought water and sandwiches and paper cups from the Land Rovers and wrapped warm blankets around their shoulders. Uncle Stoppard made me sit next to him and draped his blanket around me. In the excitement, I forgot how cold the Sahara could get at night. The glare from the three sets of headlights showed our breaths as we sat and talked about the villainous Sheridan Shakespeare.

"He was a complete madman," said Kloo, sipping her third cup of champagne. "A maniac, a lunatic. He was obsessed with Hamlet and Stoppard's book."

"He was an out-of-work actor who thought he was the only living descendant of William Shakespeare," explained Uncle Stoppard. "Remember the e-mails we got from him, Finn? Sheridan demanded I rewrite *Into My Grave,* because he thought I had offended the holy memory of his ancestor."

"Shakespeare's dead," said Kloo.

"Both of them," Mona said, grimly.

"He tried to kill me back home," said Uncle Stoppard. He told the other writers about the poison dart and the exploding package. "It was Shakespeare who followed us here and cracked open the palm pot in the lobby. It was Shakespeare who pushed the pillar that crushed Nabi back at Mallomar. He was aiming for me. But Nabi had liked hats too much."

"Hats?" said Babette.

Uncle Stoppard figured that the mad Shakespeare pushed the pillar on Nabi, thinking he was Uncle Stop. While exploring the Mallomar tombs, Nabi had expressed his admiration of Abou's yellow hat, so Uncle Stoppard let Nabi try it on. From the rooftop where Shakespeare was lurking, the yellow hat was his bull's-eye. He assumed, wrongly, that it was Uncle Stoppard who was still wearing it.

When we had returned to the hotel, after Nabi's death, and the writers all stood silently in the lobby, mourning the death of their Egyptian comrade, something had bugged me. I had stared at their reflections in the shiny marble floor and thought something was missing. Now I know what was missing. Abou's hat on Uncle Stoppard's head.

The Desert Guard brought us more coffee and water while Zamboni filled in Uncle Stoppard and Kloo about his struggle with Shakespeare on the roof. The guards brought us donuts. Do cops all over the world eat donuts?

"When I got back to the hotel," said Zamboni, rubbing his earring, "I heard the police had found a dead body in the lobby. A hotel clerk noticed a hand sticking out from a potted palm."

"Sheridan killed him," said Kloo. "It was the man who was supposed to be our bus driver. Abdullah something-or-other."

"That's what we thought," I said. "Abou and me."

"Shakespeare disguised himself as Muhammad," said Kloo, "and took his place back at the bus. I wondered at the time why he didn't understand me when I spoke to him in French."

That's what had bugged me back at the bus! Kloo had said, "Well, of course I spoke in English! You wouldn't answer when I tried French." But Muhammad, as a true Occan, should have understood French. Kloo shouldn't have had to speak to him in English.

"He had this all planned out?" asked Babette.

"Most of it," said Uncle Stoppard. "His major plan was to stay close to me. To kill me."

"He was a master of disguise," said Kloo. "And a master of improvisation. After all, he was an actor. More champagne, darling? Thank you."

"His original plan, after the fiasco at the Mallomar Tombs, was to follow us to Aznac and kill me there." Uncle Stoppard took a bite of his sandwich. "In Aznac, he would have been able to disappear more easily. He definitely did not want to kill me here in Mortville. Too few suspects. He was sure he would be discovered."

"And he was," said Nada. "But he had to take the risk and kill again."

"Omar Bah?" asked Abou.

"You mean Ravenwood," said the real Omar Bah. "Poor Truman. He loved his jokes and puzzles. He was going to reveal himself at Aznac once we all arrived. He wanted the two of us to enter the room together, side by side, and surprise you all."

"Unfortunately, he was the one who was surprised," Mona said.

"Why was he killed?" Zamboni asked. "Ravenwood, I mean."

"The birthmark," I said. Then I explained about the real birthmark, and the phony birthmark, and the Muslim taboo against exposing your soles.

"That's what he meant!" shouted Mona. "Remember

when Bah, I mean Ravenwood, was in our sleeping quarters that night and mumbled something about his soul. I thought he meant spiritual soul. But he was talking about the bottom of Muhammad's foot, his *sole*."

"Ravenwood confronted the phony Muhammad that night," said Uncle Stoppard.

On the bus ride, and in the prison of Mortville, we had been accompanied that whole time not by one person in disguise, but by two. Ravenwood and the killer Shakespeare.

"How do you know all this?" asked Ota Sato, who had been listening quietly.

"I told you, darling, he was a lunatic," Kloo said.

"He boasted about his plans," Uncle Stoppard said. "He told us everything that happened. In fact, he was proud of it. He did everything for the sake of his beloved William Shakespeare."

Tradition, I thought. Dead things. He must have planted the cobra in Uncle Stoppard's hotel room, too.

Uncle Stoppard took a drink and continued. "Like I said, Ravenwood confronted Muhammad that first night in the temple. He asked him some questions in Arabic, and Muhammad didn't respond. So Ravenwood flat out asked him who he was."

"That's when Muhammad, er, Sheridan, knocked him out," said Kloo. "Conked him with a stone from the prison yard. Then he hauled him over to the guillotine and, well, you know."

"Sheridan Shakespeare discovered that the person he thought was Bah was also in disguise," Uncle Stoppard said. "When he slugged Ravenwood, his fake whiskers flew off."

"And that gave him the idea to switch his disguise," Kloo said. "Shakespeare figured that when the authorities discovered the body of a dead man disguised as

Occo's most beloved writer, they would begin a full-blown investigation. And one thing that lunatic did not want was an investigation. So, he made the body look as if it was Muhammad—an ordinary, quiet, commonplace Fuzi bus driver. Who'd care if some guy called Muhammad was killed?"

Uncle Stoppard drew the blanket more tightly around his shoulders. "He planned on Finn being able to identify the body."

"Shakespeare was buying time," said Kloo. "He believed he'd have more freedom of movement disguised as Bah. He could stick closer to Stoppard in Aznac, attend the Ruby Raven ceremony, and wait for his chance to kill him."

"Why didn't he kill you earlier?" I said.

"Shakespeare didn't plan on killing Ravenwood. He only did it out of fear, desperation. He had to keep his identity from being discovered. But that night, I had gotten up. I heard voices. And I saw what happened. That's when Shakespeare changed his plans. He decided that instead of killing me, he would force me to rewrite *Into My Grave.*"

"My blank notebook paper!" cried Mona.

"Yes, and he kept me locked up in that hidden room, working on my book."

"How did Shakespeare know about that secret panel?" asked Mona.

"From Bah-Ravenwood. Ravenwood knew a lot about the old ruins surrounding Aznac and had read stories about the ancient Romans out in the desert and about the secret passageways and tunnels found in old temples like this one. That's what he and Sheridan were discussing when Ravenwood began using Arabic to find out if the driver was an Occan or not."

"How did he know we were in Fuz in the first place?" I asked. "The Ruby Ravens are a secret. Even if he had followed us to the airport back home, all he'd know is that we were flying to New York, maybe to Paris."

"It was the telegram," Uncle Stoppard said. "Remember how I dropped it on your bed before we left?"

"That creep was in my bedroom?"

"He broke into the house after the explosion backfired. He was going to leave another bomb waiting for us on our return, when he found the telegram."

How can you outguess a madman? If Uncle Stoppard had been neater back home and tossed the telegram into a wastebasket, we wouldn't be sitting on the steps of this abandoned prison. Instead, we'd be blown to bits outside our front door in Minneapolis.

"Why didn't you yell for help, Stoppard?" asked Zamboni. "That wall doesn't look real thick. Someone would have heard you."

"I know, Brent. Sheridan thought of that, too. He said if I tried to escape, or tried calling for help, he was going to kill Finnegan."

"Me?" I gulped.

Uncle Stoppard put his arm around my shoulder and drew me closer to him. "You were on the outside with him. If I tried anything, he would have been able to kill you before I could get help."

That's why the phony Omar Bah didn't harm me in the secret passageway. I was Sheridan Shakespeare's ace in the hole.

"But Nada, why was he after you?" asked Bletz.

"He wasn't, dear boy. Not personally. He simply needed a warm body. He felt that young Zwake was on to him, so he needed a new disguise. My veil and outfit were just what the doctor ordered, so *voilà*. I woke up one night and found myself chained in a strange room.

I believe he put something in my champagne that night. And he used the same threat on me as he did on Stoppard. I didn't want anything to happen to you, dear Alexy. Or to you, Finnegan. That beast took my clothes and made me dress in this horrid robe. I believe it's one of yours, Babette."

"Morning Primrose," said Babette.

"I thought it was pink. Anyway, after he took my clothes, Shakespeare dressed up Ravenwood's old body to look like Bah again, shoved it into the bone pit, and ran back to sleep in my cot disguised as me. I knew it would never fool you, Alexy."

"I was merely waiting for the right moment, my love," said the blond pilot.

"Two deaths and one body," I said. "It looked like Muhammad and Omar Bah had been killed, but it was Ravenwood's body both times."

"Why didn't he kill you, Kloo?" said Mona.

"Disappointed?" Kloo asked.

"Um, curious."

"I don't believe Shakespeare was a mass murderer at heart," Nada said. "A desperate lunatic, yes. His real target was Stoppard here. He only killed Nabi accidentally. And he had to do something fast in order to be on the bus—that's why he killed the driver. And of course, Ravenwood threatened to expose him. Other than that, I don't think he was a real murderer. Not at heart."

"Not at heart?" said Zamboni. "There are three bodies!"

"Thank goodness there aren't four," I said. Uncle Stoppard gave me a big goofy grin.

"Or five," said Bletz.

"Do you realize," said Babette, "that he was in the police Rover with us? That . . . that madman rode with us to Aznac and sat with us while we listened to Brentano, the same person who had fought with him at Mallomar? Hmm, I better write all this down." Out came the purple pad.

"I'll bet he had a heart attack when you pulled out that cigarette, Brent old boy," said Omar Bah with a snort.

"He was a cool one," Mona said.

"A cold one," said Uncle Stoppard.

"And all because of Shakespeare," Abou said.

"Speaking of cold ones," said Mona. "I could go for a drink back at Aznac."

Babette stood up brightly. "Yes, let's go back and celebrate. I know under the circumstances we should be in mourning, but at least Nada and Stoppard have been found. That's cause for celebration."

"Thanks to Abou," I said.

"If you hadn't figured out the backward *C* on Ravenwood's foot," Abou said, "we wouldn't have known something was wrong."

"That something was afoot." Babette laughed.

Everyone was laughing, but I felt sick. All because of one stupid book. A book I never read—the Danish history book that almost broke Uncle Stoppard's toe. If I hadn't dropped that book, if I hadn't helped Muhammad-Sheridan Shakespeare off with his shoes, Truman Ravenwood would still be playing practical jokes. Nabi Neez would still be walking in his blue running shoes. The bus driver buried with the palm trees would still be driving his bus.

"What's wrong, Finn?" Uncle Stoppard asked.

"Oh, I was just thinking about . . . dead things."

Uncle Stoppard took me by the shoulders and looked hard at me. His eyes drilled right into my brain. "It's not your fault, you know. Sheridan Shakespeare was crazy. We're not responsible for his actions. I'm not sure if *he* was responsible for his actions. When you helped him off with his shoes, you were being helpful. And observant. Why, if it wasn't for you, Nada and I would have starved back in there."

"That's right, darling," said Kloo. "We write about detectives, but you were a real detective."

"Thank goodness for your memory, Finn," said Uncle Stoppard. "Have I told everyone here that my nephew has a phenomenal memory?"

Nada leaned over to me and kissed me on both cheeks. So did Bletz. I guess it's a Russian custom. Then Alexander passed me a glass of champagne, which Uncle Stoppard intercepted and handed over to Ota Sato.

"I'm glad that horrid little man is gone," said Nada. "I'm sorry if that sounds cruel, but that's how I feel."

"And poor Ravenwood," said Babette. "Oh my goodness! Ravenwood! What's going to happen to the Ruby Raven award? This will be the last one. And we'll never find out who won. Ravenwood always kept it a secret. That weird little Hyde probably doesn't even know."

Omar Bah stood up from the Temple steps and adjusted his maroon robes.

"Indeed, Truman Ravenwood was the Nevermore Society," he said. "He chose me to be the master of ceremonies this evening, a function I haven't quite lived up to, yet. He had asked me to be the keynote speaker and give the main speech at our banquet tonight."

"And?" prompted Babette.

"And," Bah said, "Ravenwood dropped a clue regarding who the winner was. He gave me the theme of my speech. It was also the theme for his practical joke."

All eyes were on the big Occan with the tiny green fooz.

"Ravenwood said that the theme of my speech should reflect the theme found in the winner's book."

"And what was that theme?" asked Mona.

All the writers held their breath.

Omar Bah looked at me and Uncle Stoppard.

"Disguises," he said. "And Shakespeare."

A Note from Stoppard Sterling

The deadly Moroccan cobra makes its home among the desert regions of Occo, Morocco, and Lesser Occo, in northern Africa. Fortunately for my nephew Finnegan Zwake (and, I suppose, for that writer who goes by the name of Trafalgar-Squeer), the Moroccan cobra is not a spitting snake. Spitters can spray their venom to distances of up to twelve feet; if I remember correctly, the bathroom at the Fuz Hôtel Splendide was only twelve feet long. The Moroccan cobra is considered the most dangerous snake known to humankind. It is not, however, the most dangerous animal. That title is reserved— at least for the time being—for insane, out-of-work British actors.

Finnegan and I have debated and discussed for many long hours the exploding package intended to delay our departure for Fuz. Why did it explode early? The best theory we have come up with so far is this: Sheridan Shakespeare arrived in Minneapolis on a Saturday afternoon, and the Sunday we departed for Fuz (it was October) was the first day coming off of Daylight Savings Time. The British have their own version of DST, sometimes referred to as Summer Time. Shakespeare probably used a primitive timer, something he could easily smuggle onto a plane, and then wired his bomb to blow up at a specific time, say 6 A.M. (DST). Perhaps

Shakespeare had called the mail-delivery company Saturday night to ensure the bomb would arrive on time. But the next day, because all the U.S. clocks went back to "real time," the package blew up enroute at 5 A.M. Many Americans forget about Daylight Savings Time. I am convinced that Shakespeare did, too. I am also convinced that Finn and I shall *never* forget it.